D1171025

Deadly
to the
Core

Also available by Joyce St. Anthony

The Homefront News Mysteries

Death on a Deadline
Front Page Murder

Writing as Joyce Tremel
The Brewing Trouble Mysteries

A Room With a Brew
Tangled Up in a Brew
To Brew or Not to Brew

Deadly
to the
Core

A CIDER HOUSE
MYSTERY

Joyce Tremel

CROOKED
LANE

NEW YORK

PUBLISHER'S NOTE: The recipes contained in this book are to be followed exactly as written. The publisher is not responsible for your specific health or allergy needs that may require medical supervision. The publisher is not responsible for any adverse reaction to the recipes contained in this book.

Published in the United States by Crooked Lane Books, an imprint of The Quick Brown Fox & Company LLC.

Crooked Lane Books and its logo are trademarks of The Quick Brown Fox & Company LLC.

Library of Congress Catalog-in-Publication data available upon request.

ISBN (hardcover): 978-1-63910-543-4
ISBN (ebook): 978-1-63910-544-1

Cover illustration by Mary Ann Lasher

Printed in the United States.

www.crookedlanebooks.com

Crooked Lane Books
34 West 27th St., 10th Floor
New York, NY 10001

First Edition: January 2024

10 9 8 7 6 5 4 3 2 1

To all the cider makers, brewers, wine makers, and distillers everywhere.

Chapter One

I stopped my silver Highlander on the gravel driveway beside the farmhouse. I was surprised and pleased to see that the house seemed to be in much better shape than I'd imagined it would be. Although I hadn't been here since I was thirteen—almost twenty years ago—I remembered it well. My great-uncle Stan had built the house himself on the outskirts of Orchardville, Pennsylvania, borrowing from whatever style caught his fancy. It was mostly a square box with a Victorian turret and a farmhouse-style wraparound porch tacked on for good measure. The clapboard siding was plain white and the porch floor was gray. It was clear from the fading colors that neither had seen a paintbrush for a few years, but it all looked sound. I'd half expected peeling paint and a sagging porch roof.

A cramp in my left hand reminded me that I was still tightly gripping the steering wheel. I relaxed my hands and wiggled my stiff fingers. The tendons loosened and I got out of the SUV and stretched. My whole body felt stiff, but thankfully the pain I'd endured over the past year was mostly gone. At least the physical pain. I still had dreams about the accident that had claimed the life of my husband. In some of my dreams, Brian survived. When I woke and reached for him, though, my heart shattered into a thousand pieces again, just like my body had. I had been put back together with screws and titanium. People told me I was lucky, but I didn't feel that way. I didn't feel lucky to have gotten T-boned by a tractor trailer and lost the love of my life. I took a deep breath and shook the dark thoughts away. I picked up my cane that I rarely used anymore and carried it up the wooden stairs to the front porch.

I retrieved the key from under the mat where Robert Larabee, the attorney handling my uncle's estate, told me he'd leave it. The hinges on the heavy oak door squeaked as I pushed it open and the musty odor of a closed-up house greeted me. I stepped into the foyer and looked around. It had seemed so much bigger when I was a child. The pine floors were slightly scuffed but the walls were the same yellow I remembered. Grandma had called it "buttercup." I felt the corners of my mouth turn up at the memory. Grandma had once shown me how to hold a buttercup flower under my chin. According to her, if the underside of your chin turned yellow, it meant you liked butter. At the time, I'd thought Grandma was magical and had wondered how she knew a flower could do that.

I ran my hand along the oak banister of the staircase I used to slide down—when Grandma wasn't looking, of course. The living room sat to the left of the foyer and I peeked in. Uncle Stan's furniture had seen better days, but some slipcovers would make all the difference. Maybe some matching drapes on the large double window. A fresh coat of paint on the walls would help too.

The dining room and kitchen were at the far end of the hallway at the back of the house. The dining room still housed Grandma's antique mahogany table, chairs, and china cabinet. The seats on the chairs could stand to be reupholstered but otherwise looked fine. I moved on to the kitchen. It had the same white metal cabinets I remembered, but thankfully there was a newer refrigerator. I was happy to see the old 1950s-style Formica and chrome table with matching chairs still in residence. A little chrome polish and some elbow grease and they'd look like new. I had eaten so many ice cream sundaes sitting at that table in the summers I spent here.

My stomach growled at the thought of food. I'd barely eaten any breakfast and it was now four in the afternoon. Since the cupboards were definitely bare, I was going to have to hit the grocery store. I'd had thoughts of touring the orchard, but that could wait until morning.

*   *   *

Miller's Grocery Emporium was located on the east end of the main street running through Orchardville. It leaned heavily on the emporium part of its name. Groceries were only a small part of the inventory. It carried everything from auto supplies to toys. There was even a section filled with bins of loose candy that you could bag and buy by the pound. It had been my favorite thing to do when I'd gone shopping with Grandma. The only changes I could see were vinyl flooring in place of the old, scuffed linoleum, and plastic grocery carts instead of metal ones. I took one of the carts and headed to the bread aisle.

"Well, if it isn't little Katie Driscoll."

I turned at the familiar voice behind me and smiled. "It's Kate Mulligan now."

"You're all grown up, but I'd recognize that blond ponytail anywhere." Rudy Miller gave me a big grin.

"And I'd recognize that blue apron anywhere." Other than being twenty years older, Rudy hadn't changed much. He still had a full head of gray hair and wore wire-rimmed glasses. I waved my hand in the air. "This place looks exactly how I remember it. I'm glad it's the same."

"Why mess with perfection?" Rudy stopped smiling and patted my arm. "I'm sorry about your uncle. Stan was a good man, and I'm glad he left his place to you."

"Thanks."

"I heard about what happened to you—about your accident."

"You did? How?"

"Stan," Rudy said. "He kept track. He always had a soft spot for you. He might have forgotten where he lived and what day it was sometimes, but he never forgot you."

My eyes filled with tears. "I didn't know that."

Rudy patted my arm again. "Everything will be okay. You're home now, Katie. Right where you belong. If you need anything—anything at all—you let me or Ruth know."

I nodded. I couldn't speak. I was afraid that if I did, I wouldn't be able to shut off the tears.

His kind smile returned. "How about we get that cart filled up?"

Rudy insisted on helping me shop. It was a good thing he did because he kept adding items that I hadn't even thought about. When I finally checked out, he insisted it was all on the house. He refused to hear my protests. I gave in and promised to have him and his wife Ruth over for dinner once I got settled.

By the time I returned to the house, put everything away, and got myself something to eat, I was exhausted and ached all over. Long days like this reminded me what I'd been through. Not that I needed a reminder. The accident and Brian were never far from my mind.

Except for my suitcase, the few belongings I'd brought with me were still in the back of my Highlander. I went outside and retrieved a box I'd marked "IMPORTANT—UNPACK 1ST" and took it up to the same bedroom I'd spent all those summers in. The old double bed had seemed huge to me back then, but it seemed so tiny now. I sat on the unmade bed, opened the box, and took out the framed photograph on top. Our wedding photo.

We had been so happy. I touched Brian's face. "I miss you so much," I whispered. "I hope I'm doing the right thing." I could almost hear him telling me not to worry. That everything would be all right. He'd tell me this was meant to be. That inheriting an orchard was fate and I'd now get to open the cider house I'd always dreamed of. *We had dreamed of,* I corrected him in my thoughts. It was what we had planned to do someday. "Well, someday is now, babe," he'd say. *But you won't be here for it. It's not fair.*

I wiped tears from my eyes with my T-shirt. It wasn't fair, but I'd make the best of it. This was my new home. A fresh start. I put the photo on top of the dresser and pulled the new package of sheets out of the box. Once I had the bed made up, I brushed my teeth and popped a couple of ibuprofen. I fell asleep almost instantly.

* * *

After breakfast the next morning, I pulled on a fleece jacket and picked up my cane that I'd parked by the front door. After months and months of physical therapy, I didn't really need to use the cane, but I wasn't sure of the terrain in the orchard. I'd rather have it just in case.

It was a beautiful April morning. Although it was chilly now, the clear sky and the sunshine would warm things up quickly. I breathed deeply as I started up the path to the orchard. The air had that earthy aroma that Grandma once said was a promise of good things to come. I sincerely hoped that was true.

I slowed my pace as I neared the first section of trees. The small orchard that had belonged to my grandmother and Uncle Stan sat on twenty-five acres of land. Apple trees filled half of the acreage. The other half was split between peaches and pears. I didn't know much at all about growing fruit—the cidery I'd managed in Pittsburgh before the accident had bought the fruit already pressed. I'd do the same here until the harvest and maybe even after that. It would depend on the variety of apples. Some were better than others for making cider.

The trees looked healthy to me, with buds that would soon burst into fragrant blossoms.

I crossed through the middle of the apple orchard to the dirt lane that separated it from the peach orchard. The manager's cabin, as well as smaller cabins for the part-time workers who would be needed later in the season, were located a few hundred yards down the road. There was a figure standing on the porch of the manager's cabin, and I waved. The man returned my greeting. Sort of, anyway. It was more like a half-wave.

"You must be Carl. I'm glad to finally meet you," I said when I reached the porch. We'd been corresponding by email, but it wasn't the same as meeting in person. "I'm Kate Mulligan."

He shook the hand I extended. "Carl Randolph." His hand was rough, and it matched his appearance. He wore faded jeans and a red plaid flannel shirt. His sandy hair was touched with gray and hadn't seen a barber for a while. "I got that barn cleaned out. It's all ready for when your equipment arrives this week. Like I said in the emails, I think a cider house is a great idea."

"Thank you. I'm sorry I've had to do everything long distance until now."

"No worries. I was happy to do it," Carl said. "Stan was a good man." He pointed to a pair of hickory rockers. "Why don't we sit?"

I leaned my cane up against the log railing and took a seat. Just then a small gray cat came out of the cabin and hopped up onto my lap. "Well, hello, kitty."

Carl smiled. "That's Blossom. Short for Apple Blossom."

Blossom purred and began kneading my thighs.

"Looks like she's taken a shine to you," Carl said. "I don't know where she came from. She just turned up one day and decided to stay."

"She's beautiful." I ran my fingers over her soft fur and she purred louder.

Carl turned his chair to face mine. "Five years ago, I had no intention of working in an orchard. I met your uncle at the café in town. We were both sitting alone, and for some reason he invited me to move to his table. By the end of lunch, we were like old friends. He asked me if I wanted to help him out with the orchard and do some things he wasn't able to do anymore. It didn't seem to matter to him that I didn't know all that much about orchards. I was between jobs so I figured I'd give it a couple of weeks until I found something better."

"But you're still here," I said. "What made you stay?"

He shrugged. "Turned out I actually liked it. And I liked your uncle."

"Thank you for being there for him."

Carl nodded. "Not that I like to toot my own horn, but I'm good at this job. It's one of the few small orchards that's making a profit."

That caught me by surprise. Robert Larabee had mentioned that the orchard wasn't doing all that well. "Really? The attorney didn't seem to think it was."

"You know how those lawyers are," Carl said. "I'm not saying it's not hard to compete with the big corporate orchards. We can't sell the fruit as cheap as they do."

"But you can still sell it."

"Yeah. Mostly at farmers markets and the like, local restaurants and some specialty places. That's one reason your cider house is such a great idea."

"I see what you mean."

He stood. "How about I show you around and you can judge for yourself."

I pushed out of the rocker and set Blossom down on the chair. "I was hoping you'd say that." I followed Carl through the peach orchard while he filled me in on the what his job entailed—from making sure the trees got enough in the way of nutrients and water to hiring the seasonal workers needed every summer and fall. We crested a small hill and Carl pointed to a barn that was set back about two hundred feet from the roadway.

"There it is," he said.

I wanted to run ahead like I had as a child, and I would have if there hadn't been titanium holding my right leg together. When we reached the barn, I could see how much work Carl had put into it. He'd done a lot more than just clean it out. The barn I'd played in as a child had been gray and weathered, with boards missing here and there. There were no boards missing now. It was painted a beautiful muted red, with a black metal roof. The sliding barn door was charcoal gray, and it looked like it had all new hardware. I felt tears forming in my eyes. "It's beautiful," I said.

Carl smiled, his eyes crinkling at the corners. "Stan would have approved. He'd been wanting me to clean that out for two years. Wait till you see the inside." He slid open the door.

In place of the dirt floor I remembered from my childhood stood a huge empty space with insulation on the walls and a polished concrete floor. "Oh my." That was all I could come up with.

"I take it you like it."

"I love it. It's perfect. You really went above and beyond. I had no idea you were going to do all this. I thought you'd just sweep it out and I'd do the rest. I won't have much to do to get the cidery up and running." I suddenly realized his restoration efforts must have cost him a fortune. "How did you pay for all this? I must owe you a lot—besides my undying gratitude."

Carl shrugged. "I figured you'd pay me back when you could. Most of this was done by people who knew your uncle anyway. Stan was good to them and they wanted to return the favor. And folks around here loved your grandma too. Everyone wanted to help."

"As soon as we get back, I'll write you a check."

"No rush. I ain't going nowhere." He paused. "If you want me to stay on, that is."

"Of course I do. I wouldn't have it any other way."

I could see the relief in his eyes. "I'm glad to hear that," he said. "There's still work to be done in here. Jack Riggs is a local plumber, and he ran water lines and a line to the septic, but I didn't know what all you'd need in here. There's also radiant heat in the floor, so you'll be able to be open all year round. I wasn't sure what you'd want on the walls." He grinned. "I could have asked, but I wanted you to be surprised."

"You've done more than enough," I said. "I can't tell you how much I appreciate all this."

He nodded. "And I'll still help with whatever you need here." He paused for a second. "Stan would have been proud of you."

"Thank you."

"If you're okay here, I got to get back. I have about an acre of pear trees to check today."

I assured him I'd be fine. I stood for a few minutes taking in the space, wishing I'd brought a measuring tape. To get a rough measurement, I paced the length of the barn, and then the width. Not entirely accurate, but it would give me a general idea of size. I took out my cell phone and put the measurements into my notepad. When I finished that, I used the phone to take some quick snapshots and made a plan.

The fermentation tanks and the other equipment for making cider would go in the far left corner of the barn. The bar and taps at the back center. In addition to the tables and chairs I'd already ordered, I'd put picnic tables outside for the nice weather. I'd need a man door somewhere for use in the cooler weather when I'd want to keep the barn door closed. I'd need to decide what to put on the walls—I liked the idea of some type of wood—after all, it was a barn. I'd also need a restroom. My plan was to be up and running as soon as possible.

For the first time in months, I felt something like hope. I'd never completely get over my loss, but maybe things were getting better. Maybe I had a future after all. I took one last look around, then closed the barn door behind me. I smiled all the way back to the house.

Chapter Two

I was back at the house before I realized I'd left my cane on the porch of Carl's cabin. I wasn't about to make the trek back to get it. I'd been doing well without it, so I'd pick it up another day. At the moment, my growling stomach told me it was past lunch time, so I figured I'd head into town and introduce myself to a few people and grab a bite to eat at the same time.

Margie's Morsels had been a staple in town all the way back when I spent my first summer with my grandmother. Back then, "Margie" had been Margaret Yost. The current "Margie" was Marguerite Yost, Margaret's daughter. We'd kept in touch on and off over the years, but I hadn't seen her since we used to play in the creek behind her mother's house. Mrs. Yost once jumped about three feet in the air when we showed her the bullfrog we'd caught.

When I entered the café, I recognized Marguerite immediately. She was waiting on one of the tables and her back was to me, but I'd know that red hair anywhere, even though she'd ditched her child-hood pigtails for a messy bun on top of her head. The restaurant, however, looked nothing like I remembered. The old, vinyl, diner-like booths were gone, as well as the rickety tables and chairs. The new décor was a mix of rustic and modern. The old flooring had been replaced with porcelain tile that resembled hard-scraped wood planks, and the walls were painted a warm coral. Where the booths once stood now sat bleached oak tables and chairs. Instead of the long, old counter with stools, there was now a smaller counter area with a barista station that would rival anything you'd find in a big city café. Beside it was a glass case filled with bakery items.

Although it was past lunchtime, many of the tables were still occupied. I made my way to the front where there was an empty stool at the small counter. The aroma of freshly ground coffee beans was heavenly. I breathed it in and picked up a menu.

Marguerite came around the corner of the counter. "Welcome to—"Her green eyes widened as recognition set in. "Katie!" She leaned over the counter and hugged me. "I knew you were coming, but why didn't you tell me you were here? When did you get in? How's the farmhouse?"

I laughed. "Whoa. Slow down a minute. One question at a time!"

"Sorry." She grinned. "I'm just so thrilled to see you. It's been way too long. Social media posts and text messages just aren't the same thing."

"They're not, but we'll have plenty of time now."

She squeezed my hand. "I'm so sorry about Stan. He was a wonderful man."

"So I hear."

"How are you otherwise?" Marguerite asked. "I don't want to pry, but when you want to talk . . ."

I blinked away the tears that formed unexpectedly. It seemed that was happening a lot since I'd arrived. "Thank you. It's getting better every day."

Marguerite noticed the menu in my hand. "You don't need that. I know exactly what I'm making you for lunch."

"Your mom's specialty?"

"You got it," Marguerite said. "Although my version is a little more upscale."

While Marguerite went to the kitchen, her barista, who introduced himself as Noah Fisher, fixed me the special of the day—an iced cold brew with vanilla cream and chocolate shavings on top.

"You and Marguerite have known each other a long time, haven't you?" Noah said as he set my drink on the counter in front of me.

"I used to spend summers here as a kid. Your boss and I got into all kinds of trouble."

Noah smiled, showing off a dimple on his clean-shaven cheek. The few male baristas I'd known in Pittsburgh all had beards and ponytails. Noah was the opposite. His brown hair couldn't have been much shorter unless he actually shaved his head. "That doesn't surprise me where Marguerite is concerned. You don't look like a troublemaker, though."

I laughed. "I'm not sure what a troublemaker is supposed to look like, but I've mellowed over the years."

Just then, Marguerite pushed through the swinging door from the kitchen with a large platter. "Here you go."

It looked delicious. Grilled cheese made with thick slices of whole grain bread, alongside sweet potato fries and a bowl of tomato bisque. Definitely more upscale than grilled cheese with white bread and plain French fries. I took a bite of the sandwich. "Yum," I said after I swallowed. "What kind of cheese is in here?"

"Three kinds, actually," Marguerite said. "Gouda, Havarti, and sharp cheddar. And instead of butter on the bread, I use a dill aioli."

"This may be the best grilled cheese I've ever eaten."

Marguerite laughed. "I think you're just hungry."

She excused herself to check on her other customers, and I ate my lunch in silence, savoring every bite. The sweet potato fries and tomato bisque were every bit as good as the sandwich. By the time Marguerite returned, my plate was clean.

"How about some dessert?" she asked.

I groaned. "I couldn't possibly eat another thing."

"Not even a slice of pie?"

"It's tempting, but I really can't."

Marguerite grinned. "Apple pie. It's Mom's recipe. You can't turn that down."

Noah came up behind her and rested a hand on her shoulder. The gesture told me their relationship was more than just employer–employee. Good for her. She'd gone through a divorce two years ago when her husband of ten years dumped her. "You might as well give in, Kate. She's not going to stop."

"How about a slice to go? I'll eat it later."

"Deal." Marguerite looked up as the door opened. "Hi, Daniel."

"Hey, M," he said. "Is my order ready?"

Marguerite waved him over. "I have someone I want you to meet. Katie, this is Daniel Martinez. He owns the orchard next to yours. Daniel, this is Kate Mulligan."

Daniel Martinez was what my grandmother would have called a "tall drink of water." His black hair with a hint of a wave was cut short. He wore faded jeans and a denim shirt with the sleeves rolled up to his elbows.

He smiled as we shook hands. "I've heard a lot about you. Welcome to the neighborhood."

"Thanks," I said.

He slid onto the stool beside me. "I'm sorry about Stan. He was a good man and a good friend. He spoke highly of you."

"He did?"

"All the time."

"That surprises me, but maybe it shouldn't. All those years apart and I never knew he thought of me at all."

"I'm glad he decided to keep the orchard in the family," Daniel said. "I hear you're planning on opening a cider house."

"I am. Carl Randolph showed me around today, and showed me all the work that was done on the old barn. I have so many people to thank."

"You'll find that folks around here are always pitching in to help each other."

"I really appreciate it. More than anyone knows."

Marguerite set my to-go bag on the counter, and a larger bag in front of Daniel. "Did Daniel tell you how much he helped Stan over the last couple of years?"

"No, he didn't," I said.

Daniel shrugged. "I only did what any neighbor or friend would do."

"He did more than that," Marguerite said. "He and Carl managed everything when your uncle was no longer able to."

"Let it go, M. You're embarrassing me." Daniel turned to me. "We take care of each other around here. If it hadn't been me, someone else would have stepped in."

I wasn't sure I believed that, but I didn't press the point. Marguerite would fill me in later. "Thank you for whatever you did."

"Tell me about your cider house," he said, changing the subject.

While Marguerite went to wait on customers, I gave him a bit of my history—how I had managed a cidery in Pittsburgh and had thoughts of opening my own place for a long time. When I learned Uncle Stan had passed and left his property to me, I decided to move here. I left out any mention of the accident. I didn't know what Marguerite might have told him, but I wasn't ready to talk about it with a total stranger, no matter how nice he was. That was what my therapist had been for.

When I finished, Daniel said, "If you need any help with anything, don't hesitate to call me."

"Okay."

"I'm serious. Here, let me give you my number."

I retrieved my phone from my purse and entered the number he gave me.

"Put it in your speed dial."

I gave him a look but he didn't flinch. I added the number to my favorites list.

"I expect you to use that," he said. "M told me about your accident, so I know you're going to need some help now and then."

I felt my cheeks reddening. I hated that people thought I was helpless. Over the last year, I'd learned I was anything but. "I'll be fine."

Daniel's phone rang then and I was glad for the interruption. He put a twenty dollar bill down on the counter as he checked the display. "I have to get this. I'll talk to you later."

"It was nice meeting you," I said to his back as he crossed the room and strode out the door.

Marguerite returned and we chatted for a few more minutes. We made plans to get together that evening at my house to catch up. I waved to Noah on the way out. I had planned to stop at a few other stores after lunch, but I was suddenly exhausted. I'd check them out later. At the moment I was in dire need of a nap.

* * *

I poured prosecco from the bottle Marguerite had brought into two juice glasses and handed one to her. "Sorry about the glasses. This was all I could find."

"No problem. It still tastes the same."

We moved to the living room and sat down on Uncle Stan's well-worn furniture.

"Wow," Marguerite said. "This room hasn't changed much. Between the kitchen and this room, I feel like we stepped back in time."

"I know. I was glad to see the old kitchen table, but this room is going to need some work."

Marguerite raised her glass. "Cheers."

I did the same and took a sip.

After a moment, Marguerite said, "So how are you really?"

"I'm okay."

She gave me a look that would have made my grandmother proud.

"It's been hard," I finally said. "I don't like to think about it, let alone talk about it. I know that's not healthy—at least that's what my former therapist told me. Most days I'm fine." I gave her a small smile. "Today was pretty good."

"You'll have more good days."

"I know," I said. "This may sound dumb, but when I have a good day I'm afraid I'll forget Brian. I don't ever want that to happen."

"Katie, just because things get easier and the pain lessens doesn't mean you'll forget him. You were married for what? Ten years?"

"Twelve and a half." I sighed and took a sip of my wine. "It wasn't nearly long enough. Sometimes I get so angry I could scream. Why Brian and not me? If I had been the one driving . . ."

"I'm not going to tell you there's a reason for everything. I think that's a bunch of BS," Marguerite said.

"So I should just accept it and move on?"

"Is that what your therapist told you?"

"More or less," I said.

Marguerite drained her glass. "Well, your therapist is a moron."

I laughed for a moment and then got serious. "He's not a moron, but talking to you today has done more than six months of weekly sessions with him."

"You should have moved here sooner." Marguerite refilled our glasses and raised hers again. "Here's to your cider house."

I clinked my glass on hers. "Here's to rekindling old friendships and starting a new life."

We finished the bottle and talked until almost midnight. I knew the next day I might feel guilty for being happy, but that night I savored it. I fell into bed feeling more content than I had for a long while, certain for the first time that I'd made the right decision.

Chapter Three

Attorney Robert Larabee's office was on the first floor of a building in a new office park located halfway between Orchardville
and Gettysburg. When I heard the term office park, I had imagined a
large complex with many buildings like those in Pittsburgh. The only
similarity here was the glass and steel structure. The three small two-
story structures looked grossly out of place in the wooded landscape
surrounding them. The asphalt parking lot was huge, dwarfing the
fewer than a dozen cars parked there.

The interior of the attorney's office wasn't what I'd expected either.
Considering the glass and steel outside, I'd pictured sleek and modern
inside, but the opposite was true. The reception area was paneled with
dark oak wainscoting and creamy ivory walls. Two wing chairs uphol-
stered in a red and cream striped fabric flanked a small end table near
the window. My sandaled feet sank into the plush red carpeting.

A woman sitting at a large oak desk looked up as I entered. She
stood and came around the desk. "You must be Mrs. Mulligan," she
said. "I'm Cindy Larabee."

Cindy was a paralegal and the wife of Robert Larabee. I'd spoken
to her on the phone several times. She was a petite woman with
shoulder-length hair. The caramel color and highlights probably cost a

fortune to maintain. Her ash gray suit looked custom made, and I was sure her sky-high heels were some designer brand. I felt downright dowdy in my short denim skirt and T-shirt.

"Call me Kate, please," I said as we shook hands.

"Then you must call me Cindy. Have a seat and I'll tell Robert you're here."

I'd hardly sat down when she returned and showed me into her husband's office. Although the attorney and I had had many phone conversations, this was our first meeting. He was as tall as his wife was petite—well over six feet. He was also much older than his wife. Cindy appeared to be in her thirties like me, but he had to be closer to sixty—maybe older. He was well-groomed, but the string tie and cowboy boots seemed out of place with his black suit. All he needed was a cowboy hat and he'd look like he stepped off the set of *Dallas*.

He greeted me warmly and took both my hands in his. "I'm so happy to finally meet you in person. Your great-uncle was very fond of you."

"Thank you, Mr. Larabee. I only wish I had known it while he was still alive. I don't understand why he didn't keep in touch."

"It's Robert." He gestured to a chair in front of his desk and I sat down. He took a seat on the other side of the desk. "Honestly? I don't know. I'm sure Stan had his reasons." The attorney opened a folder. "I'll try to make this as painless as possible," he said. "You've already signed a number of papers, so this won't take long. These are the final real estate documents that will put everything in your name."

The next ten minutes were spent with him explaining and me signing. When we had finished and he had given me copies of the documents, he pushed the folder aside. "Have you spoken to Carl Randolph yet?"

"Yesterday morning. He gave me a tour and showed me how much work had been done on the old barn. I was so surprised."

Robert leaned back in his chair. "Are you sure you want to go ahead with your plans?"

He'd brought this up before in one of our phone conversations. Back then, I hadn't been one hundred percent sure, but I was now. "I'm positive," I said. "The cider house is the first thing I've been excited about in a long time."

"Do you really think that's wise with the way the orchard is losing money?"

"Carl said the orchard is doing well."

Robert made a noise of dismissal. "Of course he would say that. He wants to keep his job."

There was a knock on the door and a man poked his head in. "You busy?" he asked, then noticed me. "Oh, sorry. I shouldn't have interrupted."

"Nonsense," Robert said. "Come on in." He made the introductions.

Ian Bradford was Robert's relatively new law partner. He was in his late thirties and his blond hair and cornflower blue eyes could have made him a movie heartthrob.

Ian slid into the chair beside mine. "Welcome to Orchardville," he said.

"Thanks."

"I was just telling Kate that she's making a mistake with this cider house thing," Robert said. "That the orchard is losing money."

"That's not what Carl told me," I said.

Robert leaned his elbows on his desk. "Carl Randolph might know how to grow apples and pears, but he doesn't know numbers. The farm is barely solvent, and last year was a good year. What if there's a late freeze? What if there's a drought? Or an insect infestation? Taxes are going up every year. You'd be smart to sell now. Build your cider house somewhere else."

Annoyed, I mentally counted to ten before I spoke. "I'm not sell-ing. Uncle Stan left the orchard to me because he wanted to keep it in the family. I'd be betraying him to let it go."

"I get it," Ian said. "I know family means a lot, but wouldn't your uncle want you to do what's best for you?"

"That's exactly what I'm doing."

"Just give it some thought," Robert said. "I know a buyer if you decide you want to sell. I think you're foolish to hang on to it."

"I'll think about it," I said. And I would. I wouldn't change my mind, though. I'd always been a bit stubborn—Brian had called me bullheaded more than a few times. Once I'd made a decision, I stuck with it. Carl and the attorneys were viewing the situation from differ-ent perspectives, and I had a feeling Carl's was closer to my own. And frankly, I trusted Carl even though I'd only met him in person the day before. He had been close to my uncle. I doubted he'd have done so much work to get the barn ready for the cidery if he thought the orchard was failing. Even if it wasn't doing as well as Carl believed, I didn't mind hard work. And the settlement from the accident had provided me with more than enough money to do it right. I even rel-ished the idea. The orchard was my legacy. Uncle Stan had entrusted it to me and I would do my best to honor that.

* * *

I made a few phone calls, one of which was to a local ISP to get inter-net set up at the house and the newly restored barn. I was astonished to find out that Carl had already contacted them and they'd be there the next day to set everything up. Next I called Jack Riggs, the plumber, and he agreed to meet me at the barn in an hour. I hurriedly ate a sandwich and headed out to meet him.

As I passed the apple orchard, I waved to Carl, who was spraying something on one of the trees. In one of our discussions, he had told me he only used natural products for disease control. I liked that he—and I supposed Uncle Stan before him—didn't use toxic chemicals. There were enough toxins in the world, and I certainly didn't want them in my cider. A minute later, I crested the small hill and the barn came into sight.

I hadn't decided on a name for the cider house yet, but as I approached and saw the way the sunlight illuminated the color of the barn, it came to me. *Red Barn Cider Works.* I said it aloud. "Red Barn Cider Works." I liked it. It was simple, and no one could possibly mistake where they were. I couldn't wait to tell Carl and Marguerite. Marguerite would get a real kick out of it. Some of the names she had suggested after we shared that bottle of wine the night before were highly inappropriate. Funny, but not conducive to luring in customers. At least not the right kind of customers.

This name was perfect. I picked up my pace and threw open the sliding door. I'd brought a measuring tape with me, and by the time I had measured and placed some blue tape on the floor where I thought the restroom would be, I heard a vehicle on the gravel outside.

The man smiled as he entered the barn. "You must be Kate Mulligan." He reached out a hand. "I'm Jack Riggs."

I wasn't sure what I'd expected, but Jack looked more like a biker than a plumber. His mousy brown hair was pulled back in a low ponytail that reached halfway down his back. His handlebar mustache was impressive. He wore jeans and a white T-shirt with a denim jacket and motorcycle boots. A red bandanna folded into a headband completed the look.

I shook his hand. "Thanks for coming on such short notice."

"No problem," he said. "It's kind of a slow week for a change." His gaze took in the room. "This is gonna be a nice place."

"I hope so." I showed him where I wanted the unisex restroom and where I needed plumbing run for the tanks, then where I needed water and sinks for the bar. We measured and taped the floor in those areas. We also discussed running the lines for the glycol cooler that circulates glycol through the outer lining of the fermentation tanks to keep the cider at a constant temperature.

"Definitely doable," Jack said. "The area you picked for the john is the same spot I figured. I don't know if you noticed the drain cover, but that's where your commode will be. When do you want me to start?"

"As soon as you're able," I said. "My equipment is being delivered on Friday, and my goal is to be up and running in eight weeks."

He grinned. "Piece of cake. I'll start right now if you want. I just have to run to the store for a few things."

"Are you sure?" I asked. "I don't want to take you from any other jobs."

"Like I said, it's a slow week. Besides, Stan was a good guy."

It looked like I could add one more person to the Uncle Stan fan club.

Jack and I came to an agreement about cost, which was under what I'd expected, and he left to pick up the supplies. I took a few more measurements and estimated what I'd need to complete the walls and add a man door and better lighting. I'd ask Carl who did the other electric work. When I was satisfied with the list I'd made, I went back to the house to retrieve my SUV. I had some shopping to do.

* * *

The first lumberyard that came up in the search on my phone was Thompson Hardware and Lumber, about five miles away. I parked in the gravel lot and headed for the store that sat in the middle of the yard. A bell on the door jangled as I opened it and walked inside. A man stocking cans of stain looked up and headed my way.

"Can I help you find anything?" he asked.

"Probably. I need to order a bunch of stuff."

"Come on over to the desk and we'll get started."

As we crossed the store to the counter in the back, I noticed he kept looking at me. He crossed to the other side of the counter and motioned for me to take a seat.

He sat down and picked up a notebook and pen. "I don't mean to be rude," he said, "but you look really familiar. Do I know you from somewhere?"

I shook my head. "I don't think so. I just moved here. I used to spend summers in the area when I was a kid, though."

He grinned suddenly. "That's it! You hung around with Marguerite Yost, didn't you?"

"I did." I studied his face, but I still couldn't place him.

"You might not remember this, but when I was about ten, I jumped into the deep water at Simmons Lake to impress Marguerite even though I couldn't swim. You dove in and pulled me out."

"I remember that!" I said. "That was you?" I recalled the incident, but time had dulled my memory of what the kid had looked like.

"Unfortunately. And it made no impression whatsoever on Marguerite except that maybe she thought I was an idiot."

I laughed. "Everyone's an idiot at ten. I'm sure you're far from it now."

"My wife isn't so sure sometimes," he said with a smile. "Anyway, I'm Mike Thompson."

"Kate Mulligan. Is this your store?" I asked.

"Yep. It is now. My dad sold his farm a few months ago, but he wanted to keep the store in the family. He deeded it to me, and he and my mom moved to New Mexico. They always wanted to see the west and now's their chance."

"That's great."

"So what are you looking for?"

I told him about the cider house and what had been done already. He took down the measurements I'd brought with me, then we went out to the yard to look at some of the lumber. After spending a good thirty minutes looking at various boards, I chose some half-inch rough-sawn pine for the walls. Back inside, Mike showed me some corrugated tin panels that I decided would look perfect skirting the bar. I also ordered a steel man door and some locks. At the last minute I added on a small air compressor and a nail gun. No sense hammering all that wood by hand. I tried not to wince at the total—not that it mattered. I had more than enough from the accident settlement. Mike said delivery would be the day after tomorrow. I decided to take the compressor, nail gun, and two-by-fours with me, hoping to get the bathroom framed before the delivery on Thursday. I'd have plenty of time to get the boards on the walls before the tables, chairs, and barstools that I'd ordered from a woodworker friend arrived. Everything was moving right along.

* * *

I didn't feel like making anything for dinner so, after a short rest, I went into town. Marguerite's place closed every day at three, but there was a tavern on the main street that was supposed to have good food. There were only a few parking spots on the street, so I squeezed into one, thankful that I was an expert at parallel parking after living in Pittsburgh most of my life. I grabbed my purse and my phone and jaywalked across the street.

The restaurant had the imaginative and innovative name of The Tavern. I studied the place while I stood by the *Please Wait to Be Seated* sign. The décor was as boring as the name. The hardwood floors and the tables, chairs, and booths were all the same light color, as were the blinds on the windows. The walls were painted beige. Even the acoustic ceiling tiles were beige. The only color in the place came from the hanging lights over each booth—they were a bright orange. If the food turned out to be beige as well, I was leaving.

The hostess appeared and I confirmed I was a party of one. She lifted a plastic-covered menu from a rack and I followed her across the room. As we walked through the restaurant I heard a voice say "Kate."

It was Daniel. He and Carl were seated in a booth next to the window. "Why don't you sit with us?" he said.

"I don't want to interrupt," I said. "I don't mind eating alone."

"Don't be ridiculous," Carl said. "You're not interrupting anything."

Daniel stood. "Come on. Slide in here."

The hostess handed me the menu and I slipped into the booth. "Are you sure I'm not imposing?"

Daniel sat down beside me. "Not at all. As a matter of fact, we were just talking about you."

"Uh-oh," I said. "That doesn't sound good."

Carl smiled. "Not to worry. We were talking about your cider house."

"I ran into Jack Riggs," Daniel said. "He told me he was working on some plumbing there this afternoon."

"Yeah." I filled them in on the work I'd asked Jack to do.

A waiter brought Daniel and Carl each a beer and asked what I was having. He went through the draft selection and I picked a brown ale. While I checked the menu, I told them about my trip to the lumberyard and what I had ordered, and that I'd dropped off a compressor and two-by-fours at the barn that afternoon. I had the sore muscles to prove it.

"Who's framing the bathroom and installing the boards?" Daniel asked.

I pushed the menu aside. "I am."

"You?" Carl and Daniel said in unison.

"Don't sound so surprised," I said. "My husband and I bought an old row house in Pittsburgh after we were married. We gutted the place and started over." I had loved that house, but it hadn't been the same without Brian. I sold it to one of my cousins who had just gotten married, and they were thrilled to be living there. "I wield a pretty mean nail gun."

They looked skeptical.

"If you're worried that I can't handle it, don't be. I know when I need to take a break. I'm perfectly capable of nailing some boards to the walls."

"I'll help you," Daniel said.

"I will too," Carl added.

I shook my head. "I need you to focus on the orchard, Carl. And Daniel, you have an orchard of your own to take care of."

"That doesn't mean I can't help," Daniel said. "I have plenty of free time."

"I don't want to take you away from anything. Besides, I can manage it myself."

Carl gave me a look.

"What?" I said.

"It ain't my place to say this, but I'm gonna say it anyway. You need to learn to accept help when it's offered. People around here get offended quick if they think you're snubbing them."

"I'm not snubbing anyone. I just don't want to be a bother."

Carl shook his head. "You're just like Stan. I couldn't tell him anything either. He hated having to ask for help. And I hear your grandmother was the same way. Must be a family trait."

The waiter came over then with my beer and we placed our food orders.

"Carl's right," Daniel said. "You need to accept the assist. I wouldn't offer if I didn't want to help." He grinned. "I'm going to show up anyway, so you might as well give me something to do."

I gave in. "Fine." I shook my index finger at both of them. "But I don't tolerate any slackers."

They both laughed. "Yes, ma'am," Carl said.

While we ate, I went over with them what needed to be done. Maybe this accepting help thing would work out after all.

Chapter Four

I was up bright and early Wednesday morning, feeling more ener-
gized than I had in a long time. The lumberyard delivery wasn't
until tomorrow and my tanks and other supplies weren't coming
until Friday, but I headed to the barn anyway to check on what Jack
Riggs had finished so far with the plumbing. Hopefully he had the
lines run where the tanks would go so I could get the wood on the
walls right away. If I could get the tanks placed in their permanent
location when they were delivered, it would save a lot of aggravation
having to put them into place later. The sooner they were hooked up,
the sooner I could start a batch of cider. After I checked on Jack's
progress, I'd go into town, have breakfast at Margie's Morsels, then
visit a few shops.

As I neared the barn, I spotted Carl and Jack standing outside carrying on what appeared to be an animated discussion. Neither one saw
me and, as I got closer, I heard Jack tell Carl to mind his own
business.

"You're being stupid," Carl said. "You're going to regret it."

Jack dug his hands into the pockets of his jeans. "You're the one
that's gonna regret it."

Carl stared at him for a moment. "Suit yourself. Just don't come crying to me later on." He turned and walked back toward the orchard.

Jack saw me and waved.

"Everything okay?" I asked when I reached him.

"Nothing I can't handle," he said.

I was curious, but I let it go. Maybe Carl would fill me in later. "How did you make out with the plumbing yesterday?"

Jack seemed relieved I had changed the subject. "Good. I think you'll be happy." I followed him while he gathered up some supplies from his truck. "I ran all the PEX lines to where you're putting your tanks and today I'll work on the bathroom. I can't really run anything to the bar area until I see what you're putting in."

I had figured as much. After the delivery from the lumberyard came, I could give him a better idea. I followed Jack inside and was surprised to see Daniel with what looked like framing for a wall laid out on the floor. "What are you doing here?" I asked.

"Building a wall. At least I think it's a wall." He stooped and raised it upright.

"Let me help with that," I said.

"I got it." He pushed it into place where I'd stuck tape on the floor to indicate where a bathroom wall should be. "Hand me the level."

I couldn't decide whether to be grateful he was helping or annoyed that he was ordering me around. I handed him the level, then picked up the framing nailer. "Let me know when it's level."

A few seconds later he said, "Nail away."

It wasn't long before the wall was secured and I put the nail gun on the floor. "I didn't expect to see you here," I said.

"I told you I'd help. I didn't have much to do this morning."

"Well, thanks. But you really don't have to do this."

"I know." He picked up a travel mug and drank from it. "Did you see Carl outside?"

"Sort of." I glanced over my shoulder. Jack was on the other side of the barn. I told Daniel what I'd overheard between Jack and Carl. "Do you know what that was all about?"

"Not really," he said. "They don't always see eye to eye on things."

"Like what?"

He shrugged. "Carl's a little opinionated sometimes. And Jack doesn't take well to criticism."

"Why would Carl criticize Jack?" I asked. "His work must be good or Carl wouldn't have hired him."

"It probably doesn't have anything to do with his work." He put his travel mug down. "Anyway, Carl said to tell you that Levi Franklin will be by this afternoon to talk to you about the rest of the electric."

Jack came over then and showed me the bathroom fixtures he'd picked up the day before. After that I let them both get back to work. My stomach was growling by then, so I walked back to the house, retrieved my purse and keys, and headed to Margie's Morsels.

* * *

Noah was at the counter handing a woman a to-go coffee. He waved me over. "Marguerite's in the kitchen. Have a seat."

I slid onto a stool. "What's your specialty brew today?"

Noah smiled. "I have three. A Kona blend, a cappuccino made with espresso beans imported from Italy, and an iced chocolate latte."

"The latte sounds good but I'll take the cappuccino. With an extra shot."

"Good choice. I like that extra boost in the morning too."

Marguerite came out of the kitchen carrying two large platters that appeared to have every breakfast item known to man on them. She nodded her head to me as she passed. "I'll be right back, Kate."

She served the platters to two guys on the far side of the restaurant. When she turned to leave, one of them patted her on the bottom. She spun around and poked her index finger hard into his forehead, then leaned over and said something to him that I couldn't hear. His face turned as red as the shirt he was wearing, and he muttered an apology.

She grinned as she sat down beside me.

"What did you say to that guy?" I asked. "I'm surprised you didn't deck him."

"That's Lonny Interthal. I'm friends with his wife. I told him if he ever did that again I'd not only tell Lisa, but he'd be singing soprano for the rest of his life."

I laughed. "It seemed to work."

"What can I get you?" Marguerite asked.

"Just some scrambled eggs and toast."

"Coming right up." She stood and headed through the door to the kitchen.

Noah brought my cappuccino, and I sipped it as I looked around the restaurant. I didn't know a soul there. A young couple held hands across their table, and a pang of sadness went through me. I know Brian would have told me to get over it and move on, but it wasn't easy. I wasn't sure I'd ever get over feeling guilty that I was alive and he wasn't. And I wasn't sure I wanted to get past it. He was a part of me and always would be. Lost in thought, I didn't notice someone taking the stool beside me until she spoke.

"You look a million miles away," she said.

"Sorry. I guess I was."

"You're Stan's niece, aren't you?"

"I am." I reached out a hand. "Kate Mulligan."

The stack of silver bracelets she wore jangled as she shook my hand. "Renee Jennings. I own the candle shop down the street."

"Nice to meet you," I said. "I've been meaning to stop in. I love candles, and I love the name of your shop."

Renee smiled. "I can thank my husband for coming up with the name ScentSations. Eli did weeks of research to find something unique that no one else was using. He's also a lot better with numbers than I am. He handles the business end, and I do the candle making. I can't add two and two together so it works out well."

Noah set a plain black coffee in front of her, then went to wait on another customer. While Renee took a sip of her java, I studied her. She appeared to be about my age, maybe a little older. Her black hair was short, and her silver hoop earrings matched her bracelets. She wore a long purple skirt and a white tank top.

Renee turned back to me. "I'm sorry about Stan. I didn't know him well. He only stopped into the store twice, but he seemed like a nice person."

"Thanks." I didn't know what else to say. I wasn't about to tell her I hadn't known him all that well either.

"So you're going to be making cider?"

"I am."

"That's exciting," Renee said.

"I think so." I had a thought. "Would you be interested in making some candles for the cidery? I'd like to put some kind of centerpiece on each table."

"I'd love to! Why don't you stop in one day and we can go over exactly what you want. I'll come up with a few basic ideas and we'll go from there."

"Great! It probably won't be until next week."

"That'll be fine."

Marguerite brought my breakfast then and handed a take-out bag to Renee. After Renee left, Marguerite said, "Daniel told me he was going to work at the barn today."

I nodded. "He was there this morning, as well as Jack Riggs and Carl." I lifted my fork and paused. "It looked like Jack and Carl were arguing about something. I asked Daniel about it and he just said they didn't always see eye to eye. It seemed like more than that to me."

"What did you overhear?"

I swallowed the bite of egg I'd just put in my mouth. "I only heard the tail end of their conversation. Jack told Carl to mind his own business and Carl told Jack he was going to regret it. Then Jack told Carl *he* was the one who was going to regret it."

"Interesting."

"It's none of my business, but I am curious," I said. "Brian used to tell me it was going to get me into trouble someday."

"You could ask Carl. Then you'd know for sure."

I picked up a slice of toast. "I could, but like I said, it's really not my business. As long as Jack gets the plumbing finished, he and Carl can argue all they want."

* * *

I spent what was left of the morning unpacking a few more things before the installer came with the internet equipment. I'd just placed my laptop on the dining room table when she arrived. Uncle Stan had already had cable for his TV, so she was able to get everything connected and up and running in the house in no time. We walked over to the barn and I filled her in on what I needed for the cider house. She made some notes and said she'd be back the next day. Unlike in the house, which was already wired, she needed to bring a crew to run the cable from the telephone pole.

A little later, Carl arrived with the electrician. Blossom the cat led the way. She purred as she rubbed up against my leg.

"Sorry about that," Carl said. "She's been following me everywhere today. Or maybe I should say leading me everywhere."

I reached down and petted her, which made her purr even louder. "I don't mind at all. Blossom is welcome here anytime. I'm going to have to get her some treats."

Carl grinned. "She'll be your friend for life if you do. She especially likes the chicken ones."

He introduced me to the electrician and we shook hands. Levi Franklin looked like he was barely out of high school. He was tall and thin, with rusty red hair and freckles.

Levi smiled. "Before you ask, I'm twenty-six. I've been an electrician for six years."

"You must get asked about that all the time," I said.

"I'm not always asked, but I've learned to recognize the look people give me. I considered growing a beard, but my wife won't let me."

"Levi's good at his job," Carl said. "You won't be disappointed."

"I'm not disappointed so far," I said. I gave Levi the tour and told him what I needed in addition to the work he'd done before I arrived in town.

"I'll get started right away," he said. "I'll work where you're placing your equipment first, then Jack and I can hook everything up when it comes."

Carl made a face at Levi's mention of Jack. When Levi went out to his van, I asked Carl what was going on between him and Jack.

"Nothing," he said.

I told him what I'd witnessed earlier. "And just now you made a face when Levi mentioned him."

Carl looked like he was weighing what to tell me.

"Look," I said. "I need to rely on you. I can't do that if you're keeping some kind of secret. And I don't need anyone fighting."

"We ain't fighting," Carl said. "Not exactly. Jack and I just don't agree on a couple of things."

"Like what?"

"You're not going to give up, are you? Must be another family trait."

Levi came back in carrying a roll of heavy-duty wire.

"We can talk about it later," Carl said. "I'm gonna help Levi for a bit."

"Fine." I watched as he walked with Levi over to the tank area. I'd let it go for now.

The rest of the day passed quickly and so did the next two days. I was much too busy to nag Carl about it again. After the delivery from the lumberyard on Thursday morning, Daniel and I spent the rest of the day nailing boards on the wall behind where the tanks would be. The delivery of my fermentation tanks went flawlessly on Friday, and by noon they were in place. Levi and Jack would hook them up on Monday.

I limped back to the house on Friday afternoon, wishing I hadn't left my cane at Carl's cabin the other day. Carl had mentioned it and offered to drop it off but I told him I didn't need it. After that, I guess we both sort of forgot about it. Until now, that is. My cell phone rang as I walked. It was a number I didn't recognize, but it was local so I answered it.

"Hi, Katie. This is Ruth. Ruth Miller in case you've forgotten me."

I smiled. "I'd never forget you. How are you?"

"I'm happy to hear your voice again. You don't sound any different!"

"I'm not sure if that's good or bad."

"It's most certainly good. Rudy and I want you to come to dinner tonight. I know you're busy, but you have to eat, and it might as well be with us."

"But—"

"I'm not taking no for an answer," she said. "We'll eat at six. See you then."

She ended the call before I could protest. All I'd wanted to do was pop some ibuprofen, take a hot shower and a long nap, but it looked like I was going out for dinner instead.

* * *

Thank goodness for GPS, because as a kid I'd paid no attention to where we had been going when Grandma, Uncle Stan, and I had visited the Millers. Their small cottage hadn't changed much over the years. It was as pristine as ever, painted a pretty shade of pale yellow. Before I had a chance to ring the bell, Ruth opened the door and pulled me into a hug.

"Oh, Katie," she said. "It's so wonderful to see you again." She held me at arm's length. "You are the spitting image of Melinda when she was your age."

Ruth and my grandma Melinda had been lifelong friends, despite Ruth being ten years younger. "I could do worse," I said. "You haven't changed a bit. Neither has Rudy." It was true. Other than Ruth's hair now being more white than black, they looked exactly the same.

"You're too kind," she said. "I hope you're hungry."

"Starving. Whatever you're making smells wonderful." I followed her to the kitchen, where she had a pot of beef stew simmering on the stove. A loaf of homemade bread sat on the counter.

Rudy came home a few minutes later. "I hope Ruth didn't have to badger you to come for dinner," he said.

"Not at all. I rarely turn down a meal that someone else cooks," I said.

Ruth ladled stew into three bowls, which she handed to Rudy. He carried them to the table while she sliced the bread. "There's butter and some peach preserves in the fridge, if you wouldn't mind getting them out."

"I don't mind at all."

"You'll be glad to know I made those preserves with peaches from Stan's orchard—your orchard. Everyone raves about Chambersburg peaches, but they don't hold a candle to yours."

I smiled. "That's good to know. I should hire you for marketing."

"I know you don't believe me, but it's true. I won't buy fruit from anyone else."

Rudy chimed in. "Ruth could run a business telling people which piece of fruit came from where."

She giggled like a young girl. "What can I say? It's a talent." She pointed to the table. "How about we eat before this gets cold?"

The meal was delicious. After we'd eaten, Ruth poured coffee for the three of us and we took our mugs to the living room. Rudy picked up a photo album from the coffee table and handed it to me.

"We thought you might like to see these. There are a lot of pictures of Melinda and Stan as well as Karen. And you, of course."

I'd been wondering if they'd mention my mother. I never knew whether she had been the one to break ties with Grandma and Uncle Stan or if they had. Any time I had asked her, she just said that it was for the best. She had died of cancer almost ten years ago now. I never knew my father. My mother had always said he'd died before I was born. "Did Grandma talk about Mom at all?"

Ruth nodded. "All the time. She was heartbroken that Karen wouldn't let you visit anymore."

"So Mom was the one who broke it off? I never knew. She wouldn't talk about it. Why did she do that? What happened?"

"It's not important now," Ruth said. "It's in the past, and that's where it should stay."

"But it's important to me," I said. "Mom would never talk about it. I'd really like to know."

Ruth and Rudy exchanged glances, then Rudy gave her a little nod.

"I don't know the whole story," Ruth said. "Do you remember a man your mother had been dating during the last summer you two stayed at your grandmother's?"

"Mom was dating? I don't remember that at all."

"She must have kept it from you," Rudy said. "Stan didn't like him one bit."

"And neither did Melinda," Ruth said. "I never met him but your grandmother said he was bad news. Karen didn't agree, even after she came home with a bruise on her face one night."

A chill went through me. "The guy hit her?"

Ruth nodded. "Melinda ordered her to stop seeing him. Karen didn't like being told what to do. She refused. Melinda gave her an ultimatum to break up with him or go home. Your grandmother never imagined that Karen would choose to leave."

"So essentially she broke up with him anyway by leaving town," I said. "I knew my mother was stubborn, but sheesh." I shook my head. "She could have reconciled with Grandma. Instead she kept us apart instead of admitting she was wrong. What happened to that man?"

"I heard he was arrested for seriously injuring someone in a fight not long after that," Ruth said.

"A blessing, if you ask me," Rudy said. "Melinda said that Karen thought that the man would follow her to Pittsburgh and they'd live happily ever after. When he didn't, Karen blamed Melinda and Stan. Your mother seemed to think she could have redeemed him."

"Wow. No wonder she never talked about it," I said. "But to harbor that resentment all those years . . ."

Ruth patted my knee.

"I wish I'd known," I said. There wasn't much point in being angry about it, but I was. "I can't believe she'd do that to me—and to her own mother. She kept us apart for no reason. So many wasted years."

"But now you're back where you belong," Rudy added. "That's all that matters."

* * *

I slept well and awoke at first light. It had been an enjoyable evening, although I was puzzled as to why the Millers didn't want to talk about the estrangement between my mother and grandmother. I was glad they had finally relented and told me the truth. At least now I knew what had happened. I loved looking through the old photos. Ruth found a picture of Grandma when she was not much older than me. Ruth was right—I looked just like her.

I had two hours before I was to meet Carl at his cabin. He'd left me a message while I was on my way to the Millers' telling me to stop by in the morning around nine—he didn't say why. Now that the cidery was well on its way, I hoped he'd give me my first lesson on owning an orchard.

Ruth had insisted I take the bread and peach preserves with me, so I made toast to go along with some scrambled eggs for breakfast. I still had some time after I got dressed, so I took a leisurely stroll to the restored barn.

After a quick walk through the barn, I headed to Carl's cabin. I half expected him to be waiting on the porch, but he wasn't. The front door was open and I could hear a radio blaring inside. I knocked on the open doorframe, but I doubted he could hear it over the radio.

"Carl?" I called.

When there was no response. I called his name again, louder this time. I jumped when Blossom tore out of the cabin. She meowed loudly and rubbed against my ankle. I reached down and picked her up. I called for Carl again. When he didn't answer I stepped inside, hoping I wouldn't catch him coming out of the shower or anything. "Carl? Are you in here?"

I crossed the room toward the kitchen, and that's when I spotted feet on the other side of the cabinets separating the living area from the kitchen. "Oh no." The hair on the back of my neck stood up as I hurried over. Still holding Blossom, I sank to my knees. There was nothing I could do for him. Carl was dead.

Chapter Five

At the sight of Carl's head wound, a vision of a shattered windshield, mangled steel, and Brian motionless and bloody flashed through my mind. A sob escaped and I sucked in air, trying to catch my breath. Somehow I got to my feet and stumbled out to the front porch, collapsing onto the top step. I put Blossom down beside me. She spotted a chipmunk and took off after it. When I could breathe again, I pulled my phone from my jacket pocket. My hands were shaking badly as I tapped 911. The dispatcher listened to my mostly incoherent message and said she'd notify the police.

I didn't want to wait alone but didn't know who to call. Marguerite would be busy at her café and there was no way I was going to bother the Millers. Robert was a good half hour away. Daniel. He'd said to call if I needed anything. I hesitated a moment, then pressed his number on my favorites list. I changed my mind as soon as it rang. I hit end.

Seconds later, my phone rang. It was Daniel. My hello sounded more like a croak.

"Kate?" he said.

"I'm sorry I bothered you. You didn't have to call back."

"I told you to call if you needed anything." He must have heard something in my voice. "Is something wrong?"

"Yes."

"Where are you?"

"Carl's cabin." I took a breath. "He's dead."

"I'll be right there," he said. "I'm getting in my truck now."

When Daniel arrived a couple of minutes later, I'd managed to stop shaking. "You really didn't have to come," I said. "The police should be here any minute."

Instead of responding, he strode past me into the cabin and returned a minute later. "What happened?" He sat down beside me on the step.

"I was supposed to meet Carl around nine. When I got here, the door was open. He didn't answer when I called his name so I went in. I found him . . ." I shuddered.

"Did you touch anything?"

"No."

"Are you sure?"

"Of course I'm sure. Why?"

I spotted a police vehicle coming up the dirt road. Daniel stood as the SUV came to a halt. I rose to my feet and swayed. Daniel grabbed my elbow and sat me back down.

"Stay here," he said. "Let me handle this." He walked down the steps and toward the road.

I didn't like being told what to do. I stubbornly got up and held onto the railing.

The officer got out of the vehicle and greeted Daniel like they were old friends, which they probably were. Everyone knew everyone here. Except me, of course. I couldn't hear what they were saying, but Daniel pointed to the cabin and the officer nodded a couple of times. In a minute or so they headed my way.

Daniel introduced us. "Kate, this is Chief Scott Flowers."

He reached out a hand and I shook it. "Kate Mulligan," I said.

Chief Flowers wasn't much older than I was. He had military-short light brown hair and wore khakis and a pale green shirt instead of a uniform. "I'm sorry to meet you under these circumstances," he said. "I knew your grandmother and your great-uncle. They were good people."

"Yes, they were."

"Tell me what happened here," he said.

I told him the same thing I'd told Daniel.

"I'm going to get my camera and take a look inside," Chief Flowers said.

When he returned from his vehicle with the camera, Daniel went inside with him and I took a seat in one of the porch chairs. I was glad he hadn't asked me to accompany them. One look at Carl had been enough. I tried to push the image out of my mind, to no avail. I hadn't known Carl that long, but his death shook me to the core. He'd been so kind to me and so loyal to Uncle Stan. Why would someone do something like that, especially to him? It made no sense.

I wiped tears from my eyes as the chief and Daniel came outside again. Flowers was wearing gloves and carrying my cane. "Do you know who this belongs to?" he asked.

"It's mine." My voice was barely a whisper. I cleared my throat. "It's my cane."

"Do you mind telling me how your cane got inside the cabin?"

"I left it here the other day," I said.

"When exactly?"

"The day after I arrived—Monday. When I first met Carl."

He held it up. A chill went through me when I saw the blood on the handle. "Is that . . . is that what . . ." I couldn't even ask the question. A wave of nausea hit me, and I bolted to the porch railing. When

I stopped heaving, Daniel put an arm around me and led me back to the chair where I'd been sitting.

Flowers didn't give me much time to recover. "Why did you leave your cane here?"

"Can't this wait?" Daniel said. "She's pretty upset."

"Not really."

"It's all right," I said. "I can answer." I told him about the accident. "I don't use my cane all that much anymore. I took it with me on Monday morning because I wasn't sure of the ground I'd be walking on. It turned out I didn't need it and forgot about it until I got home. I planned on picking it up today when I met with Carl." My voice broke. I took a breath. "Who would do something like this? Why would someone kill Carl?"

A coroner's van pulled up just then, so answers to my questions would have to wait. A man and a woman got out, and Flowers went inside with them. Daniel took a seat in an adjacent chair.

"Are you all right?" he asked.

What a stupid question. Of course I wasn't. "I'll be okay," I said.

"Scott's a good guy."

He probably was, but I wasn't up to engaging in small talk. I closed my eyes and leaned my head back. We sat in silence until the chief exited the cabin again.

"They'll be in there for a bit," he said. "Let's continue our conversation down at my office."

"Is that really necessary?" Daniel asked.

Flowers gave him a look. "You know it is."

"It's all right." I pushed myself up from the chair. "I don't mind." I'd be glad to be anywhere else.

"She can ride with me then," Daniel said.

Flowers nodded. "Fine."

I climbed into Daniel's truck, and Chief Flowers followed us into town. The Orchardville Police Department shared a building with the post office and the town council on the far end of town, where Apple Boulevard—the main drag—intersected with Peachtree Road.

We had ridden in silence, but once Daniel parked the truck he turned to me. "Scott's a good guy."

"I know," I said. "You told me that already."

"Just tell him the truth and it will be all right."

"What does that mean?"

"Doesn't mean anything other than what I said." He opened his door and got out of the truck. Puzzled at his comment, I did the same.

The chief led us through a small open area with two gray metal desks. The desks were unoccupied at the moment. He opened a wooden door that had seen better days and motioned for me to enter. Daniel followed me until Flowers put his hand up. "Wait here. I'd like to talk to Mrs. Mulligan alone."

I half expected Daniel to protest, but instead he took a seat at one of the empty desks.

Flowers closed the door and pulled a chair over to the desk for me. "Can I get you anything? Coffee? Water?"

I shook my head.

The chief went around the desk and sat down. "Want to tell me what really happened?"

"I already did."

"Tell me again."

I repeated what I'd told him earlier—that I was supposed to meet Carl, his door was open, and I went in and found him.

"What about your cane?"

"I told you that already, too. I forgot it the other day. I left it on his porch."

"What day was that?"

I was getting annoyed at having to say it all again. "Monday morning," I snapped. "The day after I arrived. Why are you making me repeat myself?"

"Just answer the questions," he said.

It suddenly dawned on me that he was asking these questions because he thought I had killed Carl. *Shouldn't Flowers have read me my rights? Maybe I should call Robert. But wouldn't that make the chief really think I'm guilty? Of course, if he already thinks that, what does it matter?*

Flowers's voice interrupted my thoughts. "Are you going to answer the question?"

"I'm sorry," I said. "Can you repeat it?"

"Where were you last night between six and ten?" He enunciated each word like I had trouble understanding him.

"I was at the Millers'. Ruth and Rudy Miller."

He nodded. "I know the Millers."

"Ruth invited me for dinner. They were good friends with my grandmother and great-uncle. Why do you need to know that?"

"The coroner estimated Randolph's time of death as sometime between six and nine last evening."

Relief washed over me. I wasn't about to be arrested for something I didn't do.

"I'll have to verify your alibi," he said. "In the meantime, you're free to go."

"Aren't you going to tell me not to leave town?"

Flowers gave me a slight smile. "They only do that on TV."

Daniel stood when I came out of the chief's office. "Everything go okay?" he asked.

"Fine." If he thought I had killed Carl, I wasn't going to give him the satisfaction of telling him any more than that. Besides, I was exhausted. "I just want to go home."

"Sure thing." Once we were in his truck he said, "Did you tell Scott you were at the Millers' last night?"

"How did you know that?"

"Rudy saw the coroner's van go past and called to see if I knew what was going on."

"Oh." I thought of something else. "How did you know Carl was murdered last night? I could have killed him this morning."

Daniel laughed. "You? A killer? Not in a million years."

"How would you know? You hardly know me."

"I can tell."

"You didn't answer my question," I said. "How did you know Carl was killed last night?"

"Let's just say I've seen a dead body or two and leave it at that."

By this time we were back at my house and he asked if I wanted him to come in. I told him I would be all right. I stood on the porch and watched him drive off. His response to my question had left me a little unsettled. I couldn't help but wonder why he was so familiar with how dead bodies looked. And I wondered where he had been between six and ten last night.

Chapter Six

I was halfway to the kitchen to get some water when the doorbell rang. I considered ignoring it but when it was followed by frantic pounding, I reversed course. I yanked the door open and was practically tackled by Marguerite before she pulled me into a tight hug.

"Oh, Katie," she said. "I just heard the news and rushed right over. It's horrible! Are you all right? Is there something I can do?"

I burst into tears. Marguerite led me to the sofa, where I sobbed on her shoulder for a good five minutes. When I was all cried out, I pulled a tissue from the box on the coffee table and wiped my face. "Sorry about that," I said.

"You have nothing to be sorry about." Marguerite squeezed my arm.

"I thought I was holding myself together pretty well."

"You are," she said. "I sure wouldn't handle it as well as you."

I crumpled up my tissue and stood. "Want some coffee?"

"Sure."

We both headed to the kitchen. I took two mugs out of the cupboard and set one under the single serve brewer, then put a coffee pod in and pressed the button. When it finished I passed the mug to Marguerite. "There's half and half in the fridge. Help yourself." I repeated the action with the second mug, then we sat down at the vintage table.

"Can I do anything to help?" Marguerite asked.

I shook my head.

"Are you ready to talk about it?"

"I think so." I sipped coffee and set my mug down. I filled her in on finding Carl, calling Daniel, and being interviewed at the police station. "If I hadn't had an alibi, I'm sure Chief Flowers would have me in the slammer by now."

"Scott is usually more reasonable than that. He obviously doesn't know you wouldn't hurt a fly."

"That's pretty much what Daniel said."

"He's a good judge of character."

"I'll take your word for it." I wasn't as sure as she was. We sat in silence for a few minutes. "Poor Carl," I said finally. "Who would do something like that? He seemed like a good guy."

"He was good to Stan," Marguerite said.

I had known my friend long enough to see from the look on her face there was more to the story. "What aren't you saying? Does it have something to do with his argument with Jack?" Now that I thought about it, Marguerite's comments when I'd told her what I'd overheard between Carl and Jack were uncharacteristically short. I should have known there was more to it.

"It doesn't matter now. The poor man is dead."

"It matters if it might have something to do with why he was murdered."

Marguerite hesitated. "I don't want to speak ill of the dead."

"Carl was my employee and he was killed with my cane. I need to know why."

Marguerite pushed her empty mug aside. "Don't get me wrong. Carl was really good to your uncle. Good *for* him, too."

"I hear a 'but' in there."

"Not really. Just . . ." Marguerite sighed. "There were rumors."

"What kind of rumors?"

"Nothing specific," she said. "No one seemed to know where Carl came from. Where he lived before he showed up in town. Some folks found it odd that he turned up here all of a sudden and immediately befriended Stan."

"What's so suspicious about that? Carl told me how he met Uncle Stan. He was passing through and had no intention of staying. Uncle Stan offered him a job and he took it. He thought it was temporary but he decided he liked it. Nothing suspicious about it."

"The problem was that Carl would never answer anyone's questions about his past. You know how people are around here. They like to gossip about anyone and anything."

"I can only imagine what they're saying about me behind my back," I said.

"That's different. You're Melinda's granddaughter and Stan's niece. You're one of us." She laughed. "That sounds kind of ominous."

I smiled. "It does. So what were the rumors about Carl?"

"They ranged the gamut from he was fleecing your uncle to he was an escaped felon. On the other side of the coin some thought he was in the witness protection program."

"So what did you think?" I asked.

"Like I said, he was good to Stan. Whatever was in his past doesn't matter. If he'd done something bad or illegal, he more than made up for it in my opinion." She stood and took her mug to the sink. "If you want to know more, you should ask Daniel. He, Stan, and Carl were pretty tight."

"I'll do that," I said, although I wondered how much Daniel would be willing to tell me. He hadn't been exactly forthcoming when I asked how he knew so much about dead bodies. And he could very well be the person who had murdered Carl. I'd have to tread very carefully.

Marguerite had to get back to the restaurant, but she said she'd check on me later. Despite the coffee, I was suddenly exhausted. I didn't want to think about Carl or anything else at the moment. I rinsed the mugs, then headed upstairs. I stretched out on the bed and was asleep in minutes.

* * *

The buzzing of my phone on the bedside table woke me an hour later. I ignored it. I pushed out of bed, went downstairs, and made a cup of coffee. I'd just sat down with the fresh brew when my phone buzzed again. It looked like the same number as before. Probably spam, but this time I answered. "Hello?"

"Mrs. Mulligan?"

I recognized the voice. "Yes. What can I do for you, Chief Flowers?"

"First, you can call me Scott. We're not that formal around here."

He sounded much friendlier than he had earlier today. "In that case, call me Kate."

"I wanted you to know that I talked to Rudy and Ruth," he said. "They verified your alibi, so you don't have anything to worry about."

I was relieved to be off the hook. "Do you have any idea who could have done something like this?"

"Not yet. But we're looking at everyone and everything. Daniel said you witnessed an argument between the victim and Jack Riggs. What can you tell me about that?"

"Jack?"

"Yes. Jack Riggs."

"It wasn't an argument, exactly," I said. "And I only heard the end of it. Daniel said Carl and Jack just didn't see eye to eye on a few things."

"Like what?"

"I have no idea."

"What were they talking about?"

"Carl told Jack he was being stupid and that he was going to regret it. Then Jack said Carl was the one who was going to regret it."

"So Jack threatened the victim."

"It didn't sound like a threat to me," I said. "It was more like a disagreement. Neither one of them was angry. It didn't make me think they'd hurt each other."

"I'll have to talk to Riggs anyway," he said. "Do you know who else might have been a threat to Carl?"

"No, I don't. I really didn't know Carl all that well, or anyone else for that matter."

"You were exchanging emails and calls with him before you arrived, weren't you?" Scott said.

"Well, yeah, but that was all about the cider house. We never discussed anything personal."

"So you have no idea why someone would kill him."

I was getting annoyed. "Apparently you don't either. Maybe you should talk to some people in town. Or Daniel. Marguerite told me that Uncle Stan, Carl, and Daniel were good friends. If anyone knows, it would be Daniel."

"Daniel was helpful, but I wanted to see if you knew anything."

"I don't."

"Thanks for your time then," he said.

"Will you keep me informed?"

"Sure. Take care."

I set my phone on the table thinking it would be a cold day in hell before he informed me of anything. I tried to tell myself to just let him do his job and that I should concentrate on getting the cider house up and running. But I also wanted to see Carl's killer behind bars. Maybe I was just used to how Pittsburgh and Allegheny County police handled things, but I didn't think Chief Scott Flowers was up to the task. I wasn't either, but someone had used my cane to murder my employee.

I had skin in the game, as Brian used to say. I owed it to Carl to see what I could find out myself.

* * *

I paced from room to room for an hour, unable to keep still. I knew I should eat dinner, but at that moment the thought of food nauseated me. Finally, I grabbed my jacket and headed to the barn. Maybe work would settle me down. The boards were in place behind my tanks, but there was still the rest of the cidery to finish.

I slid open the barn door and switched on the lights. The air compressor was still plugged in so I switched it on. While it filled I picked out some boards. I'd continue from where we left off before the tanks were installed. I turned off my thoughts and concentrated on nailing. After a while I heard a knock on the open barn door. When I looked up, I was surprised to see it had gotten dark outside. I'd been working longer than I thought.

"I saw the lights on and thought I'd see if you were all right," Daniel said. He had a pizza box in one hand and a four pack of beer in the other. "And I brought food."

I put the nail gun down, turned off the compressor, and turned the knob to empty it. "I don't want to steal your dinner."

"It's actually for both of us. I was going to take it to your house to check on you, then I saw the lights on here."

"Thanks." I was suddenly hungry. I didn't have paper plates, but there was a roll of paper towels. They'd have to do. We sat down on the floor and I opened the box while Daniel opened two cans of brown ale from a local brewery. The pizza was half cheese and half pepperoni and I chose a slice with pepperoni.

"So how are you?" Daniel asked.

I'd just taken another bite and had to finish chewing before I answered. "I'll be okay."

"I talked to Scott," he said. "He verified your alibi."

"He called me. He wanted to know if Carl had had problems with anyone. I mentioned the disagreement with Jack."

"Jack didn't kill him."

"How do you know that?"

Daniel tore a paper towel from the roll and wiped his fingers. "I've known both of them for a long time. Despite looking like a Hell's Angel, Jack wouldn't hurt a fly."

"What about Carl?" I asked. "Could he have pushed Jack enough for him to strike back?"

Daniel shook his head. "No way. Carl's not—wasn't—the easiest person to get along with sometimes, but he was a good guy. I mean look at what he did for you."

"I know. He was wonderful to me. Was there anyone who wanted to hurt Carl? What about one of the migrant workers he was hiring?"

"It's too early in the season. They won't arrive for a while yet."

"Who had a motive then?" I almost added *besides you*, then thought better of it.

Daniel was silent for a minute like he was weighing what to tell me. "Not everyone in town liked or trusted Carl. He was very protective of Stan."

"That's a good thing, right?"

"To a point. When Stan started having memory problems, Carl was worried someone would try and take advantage of him. He screened Stan's mail and anything else he could. And I know he didn't like Stan's attorney."

"Robert? Why? He seems to have done a good job handling my uncle's estate."

"I don't know. Carl wouldn't say. All he said was that you couldn't trust lawyers as far as you could throw them."

I finished my second slice of pizza and wiped my hands and mouth on a paper towel. "Sounds like it wasn't anything personal. Just attorneys in general."

"Maybe."

Daniel's phone buzzed and he checked the screen. "I need to take this." He stood and walked outside as he answered.

I closed the pizza box and pushed to my feet. I gathered up the trash and dropped it into a garbage bag.

When Daniel returned he said, "I have to go, but I'll drive you up to the house first."

"I can walk."

"I'd rather drop you off."

Truth be told, I was glad for the offer. My legs ached and it would have been an effort to walk home in the dark. I turned off the lights and slid the barn door closed. Daniel was quiet on the short ride to the house. I asked if something was wrong.

"Nothing you need to worry about," he said.

I took him at his word and thanked him for the ride. As he drove off, Blossom came out from under one of the hydrangeas at the bottom of the steps. She meowed and rubbed against my legs as I opened the door. "I bet you're hungry," I said.

She meowed louder and followed me inside.

"I'll see what I can find for you to eat." There was a can of tuna in the kitchen. I opened it, dumped the fish onto a plate, and took it out to the porch where Blossom dug in with relish. As much as I hated the idea, I'd need to go to Carl's cabin in the morning and get her food and litter box.

It looked like I now had a cat.

Chapter Seven

First thing in the morning, I left Blossom sleeping on the front porch and headed to Carl's cabin. The morning air was cool with a promise of a warm April day to come. I breathed in the earthy aroma of nature beginning to come alive again. Sort of like me.

When I reached the cabin, I was glad to see there was no crime scene tape across the door. I didn't know if the police even bothered with it around here. Part of me still wondered if Scott and his few officers were equipped to investigate a murder case. Maybe the state police were assisting. I could ask Daniel. He might know.

I paused on the porch and took a deep breath, forcing the image of Carl's body out of my mind, then opened the door and went inside. Carl's cabin consisted of one room plus a bedroom and bath. I couldn't tell if the combined kitchen and living area looked much different. There was fingerprint powder on several surfaces. Some of the kitchen drawers were open and appeared to have been searched. I wondered whether the police had done that or whoever had killed Carl. Had someone been looking for something?

I avoided looking at the spot where I'd found Carl. Blossom's food was likely in one of the kitchen cabinets. I opened the cabinet under the sink and found a container of litter and a bag of dry food.

I pulled them out. Blossom's food and water dishes were on a mat in the corner. I emptied and rinsed them, then dried them with a paper towel. I found the litter box in the bathroom and carried it out to the porch. I should have brought my car—I was going to have to make two trips.

When I brought the rest of Blossom's things outside, Scott Flowers pulled up in his squad car. I waited while he got out and headed my way.

"You shouldn't be here. What do you think you're doing?" he asked.

"I had to get Blossom's things."

"Who the hell is Blossom?"

"Carl's cat. Who is now my cat," I said. "I needed to pick up her food and litter. Is that a problem?"

"You should have called me first."

"Why?"

Scott looked as if he was trying not to roll his eyes. "Because this might still be an active crime scene."

"Is it?"

Now he really did roll his eyes. "That's not the point. You didn't know whether it was or not. You could have disturbed evidence."

"The only thing I touched was the cabinet under the sink. And I picked up the litter in the bathroom. That's it."

"Like I said, not the point. Next time check with me first."

"I seriously doubt I'll have the opportunity to disturb another one of your crime scenes."

There was a hint of a smile on his face. "Good thing." He pointed to the items I'd gathered up. "Do you need help with those? I don't see your vehicle anywhere."

I told him I hadn't driven and he offered me a ride back to the house. I took him up on it. On the way, I asked about the investigation.

"We're working on it," Scott said.

"What does that mean exactly?"

"It means we're working on it. Before you ask, everyone is a suspect at this point. We haven't narrowed it down. It's possible it was just a break-in gone wrong. It's too soon to tell."

"I noticed that you checked for fingerprints and went through some of the kitchen drawers. Did you find anything?"

"You're awfully nosy."

That didn't answer my question, so I ignored it. "Well, did you find anything?"

Scott let out a sigh. "You're not going to give up, are you?"

"Nope."

"The state police will run the prints," he said. "And the kitchen drawers were like that. They were already open." He pulled up in front of my house and we got out of the car. He opened the trunk and we retrieved the food and litter supplies and set them down on the porch. "Do you happen to know what Randolph's final wishes were?"

I swallowed the lump that suddenly formed in my throat. The thought had never crossed my mind. "I don't," I said. "We never discussed anything personal. Daniel might know."

"I'll ask him." Scott started for his car, then turned around. "By the way, that cabin is no longer an active scene. You can go in and do whatever you have to do."

I had a few choice words for him stringing me along like he did, but I kept them to myself. I watched him drive away, then took the cat supplies inside. Blossom would be happy.

* * *

I was just about to put some bread in the toaster when there was a knock on the front door. Through the glass I could see that it was

Daniel. I dusted crumbs off my hands and headed to the door. I invited him in.

"I saw Scott drop you off so I wanted to see if you were all right," he said.

"I'm fine. I was at Carl's cabin and he offered me a ride." I told him what happened. "Is he always such a jerk?"

Daniel laughed. "Scott is about as far from a jerk as you can get. He has a dry sense of humor. Once you get to know him, you'll see that."

"Dry sense of humor? The Sahara Desert is more like it." We moved to the living room and I asked if he wanted coffee.

"No thanks." He leaned back on the sofa.

"I asked Scott about the investigation but he wasn't very forthcoming," I said. "Carl worked for me. I think I have a right to know what's going on."

Daniel shrugged. "It's an open investigation. Police aren't obligated to fill you in on their progress. Besides, it's early yet and everyone is a suspect right now."

"That's exactly what Scott said—that everyone is a suspect. I find that hard to believe. Surely he can narrow it down."

"There are some suspects higher on the list than others."

"Like who?"

"You don't need to know that."

I was getting exasperated. "Why not? Carl was murdered on my property. With my cane, I might add. If anyone needs to know, it's me."

Daniel sighed. "Look, I understand your point, but that's not how it works."

"You seem to know an awful lot about murder investigations for a farmer."

"I'm not a farmer. I'm an orchardist."

61

"Orchardist? I've never heard that term before."

"You'll learn."

I was going to have to. I'd been relying on Carl to help me and now he was gone. I'd have to hire someone to take his place, but I didn't even know the right questions to ask. I changed the subject back to the investigation before I got teary eyed. "Why do you know so much about how police investigations work?"

"Does it matter?"

"No, but I'm curious."

Daniel stood. "Let's save it for another day."

"Fine." I walked him to the door. "I almost forgot. Scott asked me if I knew what Carl's final wishes were. I told him I had no idea but you might know."

"I'm sorry. I don't. That's not something we ever talked about. I'll ask around."

I closed the door and leaned on it. I was more curious than ever about Daniel's background after our conversation. On the way home from the police department yesterday—was that really only yesterday? It felt like weeks ago—Daniel seemed to know how long Carl had been dead. What had he said? Something like he'd seen a dead body or two. What could that mean? Was Daniel a former cop? He was too young to be retired. Maybe he was in the witness protection program. I wasn't sure that made sense. I wondered how he ended up owning an orchard.

I supposed it didn't really matter in the long run. The rumbling of my stomach got my attention. I headed to the kitchen to finally get breakfast. While I ate my toast, I tried to decide what I wanted to do today. My aching muscles needed a break from installing boards in the cidery and there was enough done that I could skip a day. I'd need to be there tomorrow to make sure the pipes and electric for the glycol coolant were connected properly. Scott said I could do what needed to be done in Carl's cabin, but I didn't feel up to tackling that just yet. I'd have to check soon, though, and see if he had a will or anything to tell me about his final wishes.

After I cleaned up the kitchen and threw a load of laundry in, I decided to head into town and visit some of the shops—a perfect thing to do on a Sunday afternoon. It was high time I got to know more of the local shop owners. Besides, some of them had known Carl, and might even know who had wanted him dead.

*   *   *

The bell on the door of ScentSations jingled when I opened it. The aroma from the scented candles was strong but not overwhelming. It was like stumbling onto a rose garden in full bloom. Renee Jennings was arranging silk flowers around a large pink candle when I walked in. She looked up and smiled.

"I didn't expect to see you so soon," she said. "Welcome."

"I decided to take the afternoon off and explore a bit." I pointed to the arrangement she was working on. "That's beautiful."

"Thanks." She pushed it aside. "I'm sorry to hear about Carl. It's so horrible. I can't imagine who would do something like that."

"I can't either."

"Do the police know who did it? Was it a burglary?"

"I don't think Chief Flowers knows much of anything yet." I almost said *anything at all*, but that really wasn't fair. I didn't know him. Daniel, and even Marguerite, thought he was a good cop. Time would tell.

"Well, I hope whoever did it is arrested quickly," Renee said. "I don't like the idea of a murderer in Orchardville."

It didn't seem like Renee knew any more about who could have killed Carl than I did. I fell back to my other reason for stopping in to see her. "Is this a good time to talk about things for the cider house?"

"Sure." She motioned to the empty shop. "We're not busy at the moment."

I told her what I was interested in.

"It sounds like you want a cross between rustic and industrial, right?"

"Yes."

"I have just the thing. I'll be right back." Renee went through a doorway and returned moments later. "How about this?" The object she placed on the counter was an ivory pillar candle ensconced in a black metal cage that looked almost like an old jail cell.

"That's perfect," I said.

"We can dress it up with something around the base that can be changed seasonally, like maybe colorful leaves in the fall. And I'm thinking instead of plain candles I'll make some that look like there's pieces of apple embedded in them."

I smiled. "You must have read my mind." We discussed how many I needed and the costs, I put a deposit down with my credit card, thanked her, and left.

There was a bakery next door that was closed on Sundays. Next to that were a couple of souvenir shops. It seemed like the closer one got to Gettysburg, the more souvenir shops popped up. I went in the first one and browsed assorted T-shirts and baseball hats. A bored-looking teen girl with more piercings than I could count manned the front counter. I didn't see whoever owned the store, but I introduced myself to the teen. She perked up a bit when I mentioned hard cider. Unfortunately for her, she had a few years before she'd be able to sample it. Legally, anyway. She told me her name was Olivia and her father owned the store. He was out running errands. I told her I'd be back another time.

I jaywalked across the street to Blue and Gray Collectibles. I pulled the door open and instead of a bell, a bugle sounded. A man sitting behind the counter stood. He bore a striking resemblance to Ulysses S. Grant, if I remembered my history correctly, and he was dressed for the part as well.

"Welcome! Welcome!" He doffed his hat and made a sweeping bow.

"Good afternoon, General Grant," I said.

"Ah, a lady who knows her history," he said.

"Not always. But some people are easier to recognize."

"I'll take it as a compliment that I got my appearance correct." He reached out a hand. "William Pearson, sometimes known as Sam Grant, at your service. My friends call me Will."

I shook his hand and introduced myself.

"I figured you weren't the run-of-the-mill tourist. And you didn't look like a reenactor. What brings you in today?"

"I'm just trying to get my bearings and learn what I can about Orchardville."

"You've come to the right place, then. But you're not exactly a stranger. You used to spend summers here."

"How did you know that?" I asked.

"Stan was a good friend of my father's," Will said. "They used to go fishing together. When Dad died a few years ago, Stan needed someone else to go fishing with him, so I filled in. My wife didn't mind." He grinned. "She was glad to get me out of the house. Now I stay out of her hair by pretending to be Grant."

"And running this store," I added.

"Judy helps me out here most days. She was a big fan of your uncle, too."

"I'm glad he had so many people looking out for him."

"I wouldn't have had it any other way," Will said. "I heard what happened to Carl Randolph. I'm honestly just surprised it didn't happen sooner."

I tried to hide the shocked look on my face.

"I don't mean any disrespect," he said. "I know he was still working the orchard, but I didn't like the man."

"Why?"

"Do you really want to hear this?"

"Yes, I do," I said. "Carl worked for me and was killed on my property. He was kind and helpful, not only to my uncle but to me. I know he was a little rough around the edges—"

"He was more than a little rough. I didn't trust the guy."

"Why not?"

"First, he came out of nowhere and all of a sudden he's working for Stan. Then Carl starts keeping tabs on Stan, wanting to know when we'll be back from fishing, you name it. And Shelley at the bank said Randolph was handling Stan's bank accounts. Doesn't that sound suspicious to you?"

"Not at all. Carl took over all the business of the orchard when Uncle Stan couldn't do it anymore. Daniel Martinez helped as well."

"Martinez seems like a straight arrow, but he's not from here either. Stan should have asked me or someone who's not an outsider to handle his business."

"I guess you must consider me an outsider as well."

Will shook his head. "That's different."

"I don't see how," I said. "Just because Carl wasn't related doesn't mean he was scamming my uncle. If that was the case, surely he would have been long gone before I got here. He wouldn't have kept the orchard going and he sure wouldn't have used his own money to restore the barn until I could pay him back."

Will stared at me for a moment. "Did you ever think about where he got the money to do all that?"

"No, I haven't. It wasn't my uncle's money, that much I know." Robert Larabee had given me all of my uncle's financial documents. Everything had been in order.

Will looked skeptical, but said, "I hope you're right, but I got the impression from talking to Shelley that Carl had a lot more money in the bank than what he made working for Stan. I didn't mean to upset you or anything. No offense."

"None taken." It bothered me, however, that a bank employee would blab about a customer's bank balance. I was glad I'd kept my account in Pittsburgh. I sure wouldn't be switching now. Will and I chatted a little more about his store and he showed me some artwork that he thought I might be interested in to hang in the cidery. Most of the pictures featured Civil War battles, and I told him I'd think about it instead of declining outright. Being so close to Gettysburg, there were more than enough places with that theme. I planned to steer clear of it.

On the way home, I pondered Will's question about Carl's finances. I'd reimbursed Carl for what he'd spent on the barn, but now I wondered about it. He hadn't been a flashy person and pretty much looked like he was living on his last dollar. And apparently Shelley at the bank thought the same. I knew for sure the money Carl had paid out wasn't from my uncle's accounts, but where had it come from? Could that be what his killer had been after? I needed to find out.

Chapter Eight

Although I was tired, I decided to forgo a nap and made a cup of coffee instead. I put it in a travel mug and headed back to Carl's cabin. I had a busy week ahead of me and didn't know when I'd get another chance. I paused on the porch. Although I'd been here just this morning, I was a little anxious. That morning had been a quick trip so I could take care of Blossom. I'd be spending more time in the cabin this time. I didn't think I'd be able to avoid looking at the spot where Carl had been killed. I told myself not to be such a baby, took a deep breath, and went inside.

I wasn't in a rush now, so I took the time to study the place. The main area consisted of a living room and small kitchen. A bathroom and bedroom were off a short hallway. I finally let my gaze move to where I'd found Carl. I had steeled myself for the worst, or at the very least some blood on the floor, but there was none. Puzzled, I crouched and took a closer look. Someone had cleaned the floor. Who? The police? That seemed odd to me. Things were different around here, but I didn't think they were that different. I straightened up, thankful that someone besides me had cleaned up. I wished they'd done the rest of the place, though.

A couple of the kitchen drawers were still partially open so I decided to start there. Maybe he jammed his mail and other papers in a drawer like my grandmother had. I checked them all, but the drawers only held the usual items—flatware, utensils, and steak knives. Like most people, Carl had a junk drawer that contained the usual little bits of everything: scissors, twist ties, some string. I moved on.

The living room furniture had seen better days. The style had been popular when I was a kid—orange and brown plaid with glossy wooden arms on the sofa and chair, and a matching ottoman. A small TV sat on a table in the corner of the room. There was an end table next to the chair with an ugly lamp on top. There was no drawer in the end table, so no place to hold papers.

I headed to the bedroom next, which was surprisingly neat. A simple blue quilt covered the bed, and it looked like Carl had taken care to make sure it was straight and smooth instead of just tossing it in place. I hesitated before opening the dresser drawers. I felt like I was invading his privacy, even though it certainly didn't matter to him anymore. All the clothes were neatly folded in the drawers. I even pulled each drawer out and checked underneath, a sure sign I watched too many police shows on TV. I lifted the bedspread and sheet and reached my hand between the mattress and box spring and ran my hand across it. I did the same all around and came up empty.

Surely Carl had kept important papers somewhere. The keys to his truck were hanging on a hook by the front door. I got up, took the keys and went outside. The door to the truck was unlocked so I slipped the keys into my pocket. His truck wasn't as neat as the cabin, but it wasn't a mess either. There was a ball cap and a plaid flannel jacket on the passenger seat. The pockets of the jacket were empty. I opened the glove compartment and went through the contents, which turned out to be the usual insurance and registration cards as well as a flashlight and a Leatherman multi-tool.

I closed the truck and locked it. I went back inside and sat down on the couch, not sure where to look next. It was possible whoever had killed Carl had taken all the papers. But why? I had no idea. Scott might know, but I had a feeling if I asked, he'd tell me in so many words to mind my own business. I supposed I could stop at the bank, but they probably wouldn't tell me anything without some kind of documentation that I had a right to that knowledge. I had another thought.

If Carl had a will, Robert might know something. Robert had been Uncle Stan's attorney and now he was mine. There was a good chance he would have been the one to prepare it. I'd contact him first thing in the morning. I probably should have called him yesterday to let him know about Carl. Tomorrow would have to do.

That settled, I pushed off the couch and headed home.

* * *

I woke up early the next morning, thanks to Blossom, who insisted she was starving to death and needed breakfast immediately. After I took care of her, I made a cup of coffee, and when I was sufficiently awake I showered and dressed. I wasn't really hungry but I made some eggs and toast anyway. I'd probably be at the barn all day and knew I wouldn't want to stop to eat later.

The sunrise was a brilliant red as I walked to my cidery. What was the saying about that? *Red sky at morning, sailors take warning?* I wondered how much truth there was to that saying. I hadn't listened to the weather forecast, but it sure didn't look like rain. As I crested the hill, the barn appeared more red than usual with the rising sun shining on it. It was almost glowing. I stopped to take it all in, wishing that Brian was beside me. I felt tears forming and I could hear his voice in my head telling me to knock it off, that I had to live the dream for both of us. *You got this, babe*, he would have said.

He was right. I had this. For both of us. I blinked the tears away and resumed my walk.

*   *   *

Jack arrived about an hour later, followed by Levi. I'd almost finished nailing boards to the last wall. I'd left a space where the man door would go. I'd considered cutting the opening, but decided that would best be left for someone who knew what they were doing.

"It's looking good in here," Jack said.

"Thanks. I just have to install a few more boards after I get someone to cut the opening for the door and put it in."

"I can do it," Levi said.

"I thought you were an electrician," I said.

"I am. I've also done some construction work. I won't even charge you extra." He smiled. "Except for maybe a glass of cider on the house every once in a while."

I returned his smile. "It's a deal." I turned to Jack. "That goes for you too."

"I was hoping you'd say that," Jack said.

"We have to get those tanks up and running first," I told them. We walked over to the tanks and I filled them in on what needed to be done. When they finished, I'd give the tanks a good cleaning before the pressed apple juice arrived tomorrow.

Jack and Levi had everything connected and tested by noon. I was just about to leave to pick up lunch somewhere for the three of us while Jack helped Levi cut the opening for the door when Marguerite arrived. I wouldn't have to track down food after all. She carried two large bags and a jug of iced tea inside and set them down on a stack of unused wood planks.

"I knew you were planning a busy day, so I brought sustenance." She reached into one of the bags and started pulling out sandwiches.

"How many people did you think you were feeding?" I asked. There were at least a dozen sandwiches, plus assorted chips, cookies, and condiments. "It looks like the loaves and the fishes."

Marguerite shrugged and placed paper plates, napkins, and cups on the wood stack. "Nah. I'll leave the miracles to you-know-who. I didn't know who would be here and I wanted to make sure there was enough." She nodded her head toward Jack. "I know he'll make short work of at least three of these sandwiches."

"Maybe even four," he said.

Jack and Levi each took plates and loaded them up. They poured iced tea into cups and went outside and sat on the tailgate of Levi's truck. Marguerite and I each fixed a plate and sat down on the floor.

"I heard you visited a few shops yesterday," Marguerite said.

"I can't believe how fast word spreads around here."

Marguerite grinned. "Charming, isn't it?"

"I'll leave my opinion on that open for the time being."

"What did you think of Will Pearson?"

I swallowed a mouthful of turkey sandwich. "I'm not quite sure what to make of him. He seemed nice enough until Carl was brought up. He didn't think much of him."

"Did he tell you his dad and Stan were good friends?" Marguerite poured iced tea into a cup and handed it to me.

"Yeah," I said. "And about going fishing, and how he went fishing with Uncle Stan after his dad died. Kind of makes me think that maybe Will was jealous that my uncle was spending more time with Carl than him."

"Could be."

"Will told me he didn't like Carl because he was an outsider. He didn't trust him to do right by my uncle. I also got the impression Will thought Carl was stealing from Uncle Stan."

"Was he?"

"Marguerite!"

"I had to ask," she said. "Will's not the only one in town who thinks there was something going on."

"Well, I know for certain Carl wasn't fleecing my uncle. I have all of Uncle Stan's bank statements and financial stuff. If there had been a problem, Robert would have told me."

"I believe you," she said. "I have to tell you, though, there were rumors. I heard this secondhand, but Carl apparently had a pretty large bank balance."

"Will asked me if I wondered where Carl got the money to fix up the barn until I reimbursed him. Someone named Shelley at the bank thought Carl had too much in his account."

Marguerite drained her cup and set it down. "It wouldn't be a stretch that she told him about Carl's bank balance. Shelley's a blabbermouth. You might want to take a look at Carl's statements and see for yourself."

I crumpled up my sandwich wrapper. "I would if I could find them." I filled her in on what I had done the day before.

"Maybe he only got electronic statements," she said.

"It's possible. But there was no computer in the cabin. And I didn't see a cell phone, either."

"But weren't you two emailing each other?"

"We were. And calling and texting. And he didn't have a landline."

"So what happened to his computer and phone?" Marguerite asked.

"That's what I'd like to know." I rose to my feet. "I'm guessing that whoever killed Carl has both of them. I need to have a chat with Chief Flowers."

Chapter Nine

"What can I do for you, Kate?" Scott asked.

I had been ushered into the chief's office, and I took the seat across from him. It seemed hard to believe that only two days ago I'd sat in the same chair thinking I'd be accused of murder. "It's about Carl," I said.

His only response was to raise an eyebrow.

"Since you told me his cabin was no longer a crime scene, I went back late yesterday afternoon looking for paperwork."

"What paperwork? A will?"

"Among other things." I explained what I'd learned from Will Pearson.

"And?" Scott said.

"I can't find any papers at all," I said. "No will, no bank statements, nothing. Don't you think that's a little odd?"

"Maybe he did everything electronically."

Marguerite had said the same thing. "Then where's his computer? And his cell phone? And why were the kitchen drawers open?"

"That's a lot of questions," Scott said. "I'll answer one of them. Randolph's cell phone is in evidence."

"What about the rest? A computer? Papers?"

I could tell Scott was trying hard to be patient. "Do you really think Randolph was the type to own a computer? I didn't see anything in his cabin to indicate he did. Did you?"

"Well . . . no."

Scott stood. "I want to solve this as much as you do. It's my job, believe it or not."

I got up from my chair. "I know that. I don't mean to interfere, but there are some things I need to know, like what to do with Carl's belongings and his truck. And where he wanted to be buried. I can't do any of that yet."

Scott put a hand on my shoulder. "I'm already looking into everything you mentioned. That's all I'm going to say right now. I promise I'll let you know right away when I have any news."

He walked me outside and I thanked him for his time. I couldn't tell if he was brushing me off or if he meant what he said. That was probably a good quality in a cop, but I didn't like it much. I thought of one other person who might know about Carl's finances—Daniel. He hadn't known what Carl's final wishes were, but no one usually discusses that with friends anyway. At least I never had. Even Brian and I had never talked about death or funerals or anything like that. In any case, I'd talk to Daniel again. Maybe he'd remember something.

* * *

When I got back to the barn, there was a black Escalade parked outside. I wondered who the owner was until I saw the steer horns fastened to the hood. Robert really took the rich Texan look to heart. He got out of the vehicle at the same time I did.

"I stopped at the house first and figured you were probably here when you didn't answer the door," he said.

I slid open the door. "Come on in and I'll give you the tour."

Robert followed me inside. "Wow. This place looks a lot different. You *have* been busy."

I dropped my purse onto the floor. "The tanks are ready to go. I'm just waiting for the apple juice. It's coming tomorrow."

The metal cleats on Robert's cowboy boots made it sound like he was tap dancing as he followed me across the floor to the fermentation tanks. "I heard about Carl Randolph," he said.

"I've been meaning to call you. I should have. I'm sorry."

"No need to be sorry." He pointed to one of the tanks. "How much does that hold?"

"Two thousand gallons, which is about sixty-four barrels."

Robert whistled. "That's a lot of cider. What do you do? Dump in the juice and hope for the best?"

"Hardly. It's not as complicated as brewing beer, but there's more to it than you think. These tanks are double walled. The juice and yeast go in the center tank and the outer tank is cooled by circulating glycol to keep the cider at a constant seventy degrees for fermentation." I pointed to the tubing and thermostat. "After about two weeks, the cider is racked to another tank, where I can add other fruit or just let it set for another couple of weeks."

"Then it's ready to drink, I guess," Robert said.

"Almost. It goes to what we call a 'brite tank,' where it's cooled to thirty-three degrees to stop fermentation. Then it gets carbonated and kegged."

"Fascinating. It sounds like a lot of work. Are you sure you're up to it?"

I wondered when he'd say something like that. "I am."

"I know you told me you don't want to sell, but I stopped by to tell you that the buyer I mentioned before is still very interested," Robert said.

"Well, I'm not."

"It's a great price—especially for a failing orchard. And I'd bet he'd up the ante if he saw this place."

"Robert, let me be very clear about this. I am not selling. Not now. Not ever."

"You're making a big mistake," he said. "The offer won't be there forever."

"Like I said—"

Robert put a hand up. "I get your point. I'll get out of your hair now."

"Before you go, I need to ask you something."

"Sure."

"What do you know about Carl? I'm trying to figure out what his final wishes might have been. Do you know if he had a will?"

"If he did, it wasn't with my firm," he said. "I can try and find out for you. There aren't that many law firms, and I know most everyone. Did you look in his papers?"

"There weren't any papers. Not even bank statements or the title for his truck."

"Maybe he just never saved anything. Some people don't. I wouldn't worry about it. I'll let you know if I find out anything." Robert walked to the door and then turned around. "And please think about what I said. This buyer is extremely interested."

I watched him drive away. There was nothing to think about. Uncle Stan had entrusted me with this place and I would honor that.

* * *

As I passed Carl's cabin on the way home I decided to take one more run at looking for anything that would help me. At the very least, I should clean out his refrigerator and cabinets and get rid of anything that needed to be tossed. I could donate canned goods and unopened nonperishables to the local food bank.

There were two cardboard boxes on the porch that were full of firewood for the firepit behind the cabin. I dumped them out and took the boxes inside. I set them down on the kitchen counter and proceeded to search everything like I had earlier. This time I checked under the furniture and inside the couch cushions. I still came up empty. Either Carl didn't save anything, like Robert suggested, or whoever killed him took it all.

With nowhere else to look, I headed to the kitchen and opened a cabinet. Carl's food choices were eclectic. There was a variety of canned soups and vegetables that I placed into one of the cardboard boxes, along with boxed macaroni and cheese, rice, pasta, and spaghetti sauce. A box of Cheerios was open so I set it aside for the trash. The unopened box of instant oatmeal went into the carton for the food bank. Fifteen minutes later, the cupboards were bare.

I tossed the lunch meat, cheese, ketchup, and mayonnaise from the refrigerator into the garbage bag. I poured the remainder of a half-gallon of milk down the drain and threw away the container. There was a six pack of Miller Lite and I placed it on the counter. I doubted the food bank would take alcohol. I'd have to find someone who wanted it—maybe Jack or Levi. I claimed the two cans of Coke and opened one to drink now.

I was just about to tackle the freezer when there was a knock on the door.

"Kate? Are you in there?" It was Daniel.

"I'm in the kitchen. The door's open."

Daniel came in and closed the door behind him. "You really should keep the door locked."

"I know," I said. "I just didn't think of it."

"I won't lecture you."

"Good. I figured I'd clean out while I have the time." I told him what I'd done so far and he offered to help. I opened the freezer door.

"Are you okay with this?" he asked. "It's only been a couple of days."

"I'm all right. I stopped by yesterday too and noticed someone had cleaned the floor where I'd found Carl."

"That was me," he said. "I didn't want you to have to deal with that."

"Thanks. I appreciate it." I pulled out a half dozen frozen dinners and put them on the counter. "What should I do with these?"

"Take them home with you."

"I doubt I'd eat them," I said.

"I'll take them, then. They won't go to waste." He smiled. "I'm a pretty good cook, but sometimes I don't feel like making a meal for just myself."

"I know the feeling."

"I guess you do. I'm sorry. I shouldn't have said that."

"There's nothing to be sorry about. Don't feel like you have to tiptoe around the fact that my husband died."

Daniel nodded. "I know it's difficult to talk about, but I'm a good listener."

"Thanks. I'll keep it that in mind."

I returned to my task and a minute later the remaining contents of the freezer, except for the ice cube trays, were in the sink. Some things were unrecognizable, and they went straight into the trash. There were two ice trays and I pulled out the top one and dropped it into the sink. I reached back in to remove the other one but it was stuck. I gave it a yank and it came loose with a plastic Ziploc bag frozen to the bottom. "That's weird," I said.

"What is?" Daniel said.

I dumped the ice from the tray into the sink and flipped it over on the counter. "This." I pulled the bag off the tray. Without even opening the bag, I could see the contents. I was pretty sure I'd found Carl's papers.

Chapter Ten

"I can't believe it," I said. "If these are what I think, I've been looking everywhere for them." I opened the bag and peeked in. I was right. These were bank statements. "Who in the world stores their important papers in the freezer?"

"Someone who doesn't want anyone to find them," Daniel said. "Why were you looking for them?"

I told him what Will Pearson and Marguerite had said. "Surely you've heard the rumors."

"Of course. I don't put stock in rumors though. Carl was a good guy. He worked hard for Stan. We both helped Stan with his bills, so if Carl had been stealing from your uncle, I'd have been the first to know about it."

"I know he wasn't stealing from Uncle Stan. But if he did have a large balance, where did the money come from?"

"Does it matter?" Daniel asked.

"It might have something to do with his murder. Carl must have had a good reason to stash these in the freezer."

"Maybe he just didn't like them lying around."

I gave him the look my grandmother used to give me when I'd said something stupid. "Seriously?" I said. "The only thing that makes sense is he didn't want anyone to see what was in this bag."

"In that case, you need to turn them over to Scott."

I shook my head. "I already talked to him this afternoon. I told him I couldn't find any of Carl's papers. He told me they were already looking into everything." Not exactly what he'd said, but it was close enough. "I asked him if he'd found a computer or cell phone. He said the phone was in evidence."

"Which means he's doing his job. He's probably already looked at Carl's finances and gone through his phone." He paused for a moment. "I'll tell you what. Let's go back to your house and we'll see what all is in the bag. If there's anything incriminating, we'll turn it over to Scott."

I agreed. Daniel helped carry the food bank items and the trash out to my SUV. I locked up the cabin and, minutes later, we were back at my place.

* * *

I poured two glasses of lemonade while Daniel emptied the contents of the Ziploc bag onto the kitchen table. I almost overpoured one glass because I was watching him so closely. I wanted to trust him because my uncle had, but I was cautious. He'd been helpful so far, but I really didn't know him. Marguerite trusted him, but she'd also trusted her ex-husband, so she didn't exactly have the best track record. I handed Daniel one of the glasses and took a seat.

"Thanks," he said. "You don't have to watch me like a hawk, you know. I'm not going to abscond with any of this."

I felt my cheeks redden. "Sorry. How did you know what I was doing?"

"You're very transparent, Kate. You don't trust me. Not yet, anyway. And that's fine. That's the way it should be."

"I do trust you. Sort of," I said. "But I don't know anything about you other than you're my neighbor and you were good to my uncle." I smiled. "And you're pretty good at building partition walls and nailing up wood panels."

"There's not much else to know. Nothing all that interesting, anyway." He fanned the papers out across the table.

There were half a dozen bank statements and something else. I pulled it out from between two papers. "Check this out." It was a map of some sort folded in quarters. I opened it up and spread it out. It wasn't your run of the mill map.

"That's a topographic map," Daniel said.

The map was yellowed, especially at the creases where it had been folded . "It looks pretty old," I said.

"It is," Daniel said. "The newer maps are computer drawn. See these lines here?"

I nodded.

"They signify elevation. You can tell it's older because the lines on this are hand drawn, and so are property lines. You don't usually see that on a map." He touched a spot near the center. "This is your orchard." He moved his finger to the left. "And this is mine. And here's the old Thompson farm—I think they sold it not long ago."

"They did. Mike Thompson at the lumberyard mentioned it."

Daniel pointed again. "I think this place is owned by Renee Jennings's father. And these two over here sold last year."

I couldn't make sense of it. "Why did Carl have this in his freezer?"

"I have no idea." He pointed to a spot in the far right corner of the map. "That property is owned by Morrison Agricultural Products."

"Who, or what, is that?"

"They're one of the largest employers in the area. They make fertilizer and pesticides."

"Is that safe?" I didn't like the idea of chemicals being manufactured so close to the orchards and farms.

Daniel nodded. "They make mostly all natural products. I've used some of their stuff, and so has Carl."

"Do you think that's why he had this map?"

"Who knows? Maybe he just found it interesting."

"Maybe." It was weird. If that's all it was, I doubted Carl would have kept it in his freezer. There was probably more to it, but I folded it up and pushed it aside. "I guess we'll never know." I picked up one of the bank statements. It was for December of the previous year. The ending balance was just shy of a hundred thousand dollars. It showed deposits of sixteen hundred dollars every two weeks, which corresponded to checks written to him from my uncle's account. Then on the last day of December, there was a large deposit of ten thousand dollars. I passed it to Daniel. "What do you make of this?"

"I don't know. A gift, maybe. Or he sold something."

"Did he have anything to sell that was worth that much?"

"I have no idea. Probably not."

I picked up the January statement. Besides his paychecks from my uncle, there were four two thousand dollar deposits—one each week. I handed the paper to Daniel. "Something's not right here." I checked the February statement. It was identical.

Daniel put the statements in order. The ones for September, October, and November showed only the regular activity. "Whatever was going on began in December with that ten grand."

"No wonder he kept these in the freezer," I said. "He didn't want anyone to know about this."

"Yeah."

Daniel looked thoughtful. I asked him if he had a theory.

"Not yet," he said. "But Scott needs to know about this in case he hasn't gotten around to checking Carl's financials yet."

"Agreed. I just wish I knew what was going on."

Daniel offered to take the statements to the police station the next day. I hesitated. Did I trust him enough? Uncle Stan and Carl had.

Daniel noticed my hesitation. "I'm not going to run off with these."

"I know." I handed him the statements. It was probably better he did it anyway. Scott would be more willing to fill Daniel in on the investigation. He hadn't exactly been forthcoming with me. I just hoped Daniel would let me know what, if anything, he learned.

*　*　*

Starting my first batch of cider on Tuesday morning went faster than I'd expected. The juice from pressed apples that I'd ordered arrived promptly at eight. It only took a couple of hours to transfer it to a tank and pitch the yeast. For my first batch I used a yeast that I knew to be very predictable. It had a built-in yeast nutrient and, from past experience, I knew the cider would top out at no higher than six percent ABV, or alcohol by volume. When I managed a cidery in Pittsburgh, I'd experimented with various yeasts—wine, champagne, and assorted beer yeasts. I'd do that again later on, but I didn't want any surprises with the first batch. I wanted a highly drinkable cider with approximately the same ABV as beer.

By lunchtime I had cleaned up and made sure the glycol coolant was circulating properly, so I decided to head into town to get a bite to eat. Noah was at the counter when I reached Margie's Morsels. He looked up, waved, and pointed to an empty table. I headed that way and sat down. The café wasn't busy at the moment—only two other tables besides mine were filled.

Marguerite carried plates from the kitchen for one of the tables and, after serving them, came over to mine. "I heard you went to see Scott yesterday."

Of course she did. "Yep."

"You'll have to fill me in," she said. "He wouldn't tell me a thing when he stopped in for coffee this morning."

I gave her my order and she headed back to the kitchen. She returned with lunch for the remaining table and came back to me with the iced tea I'd ordered.

"Yours will be up shortly." She slid into the chair opposite me. "So what did Scott tell you about Carl's computer and cell phone?"

"Not much. Apparently Carl either didn't have a computer, or someone took it. From a comment Scott made, he seemed to think Carl didn't have one. His phone is in evidence."

"And?"

"And that's it. He didn't seem concerned that I couldn't find any of Carl's papers. All he would say is he's working on it. I have a lot more to tell you when you get a break. Where's your help today?"

"We weren't busy so Liza left early. As long as no one else comes in, I can take a break now. Come to think of it, I own the place. I can take one anytime I want."

"Well, you'd better wait until you bring my food. You don't want me to give you a bad review."

"You wouldn't."

I grinned. "I'm kidding."

"I knew that. I'll be right back with your lunch and then we can chat. Noah can cover for a while."

A few minutes later Marguerite returned with my chef's salad. She quickly checked on her other two tables, then came back and took a seat. While I ate, I filled her in on what Daniel and I had found.

"In the freezer? Are you serious?" she said. "I remember Mom kept her medication list with her doctor's phone number and insurance information in the freezer. Supposedly the paramedics know to look there if their patient is unconscious or something. I've never heard of keeping anything else in there."

"I've never heard of the paramedic thing either," I said. I told her about the large deposits to Carl's account.

"Can you talk to the bank?" Marguerite asked. "If you get Shelley, she might be able to shed some light on it."

I shook my head. "She doesn't know me. I doubt she'll be as forthcoming with me as she is with someone she knows. The bank will certainly give the information to the police, but I'm not counting on Scott to tell me anything. Daniel is going to turn over the statements, so Scott might let him know what's going on."

"Daniel won't keep you in the dark."

Renee Jennings came in then and Marguerite got up. "I'll be right back. I have to get Renee's take-out order."

"I'll take care of it," Noah called over.

Marguerite plopped back into her seat.

I told her about Robert Larabee stopping to see me to say he was sorry about Carl. "He mentioned again about someone wanting to buy my property. I told him no, of course. He insisted I think about it."

"You're not, though. Right?"

"I'm not going anywhere. Don't worry."

Noah gave Renee her order and she came over to the table. "I wasn't eavesdropping, honest, but did you say you got an offer to buy your orchard?"

"I did. But I'm not selling."

"My father owns a farm not far from you. He just got an offer for his property too. Completely out of the blue."

Chapter Eleven

"Who was the offer from?" I asked.

"I don't know," Renee said. "Dad only told me about it last night. He said his lawyer dropped off some papers for him. It's really weird that you'd get an offer at the same time."

If I remembered correctly what Daniel had said, other farms and orchards in the area had also received offers or had been sold. It was definitely out of the ordinary. "Did your father tell you who made the offer?"

Renee shook her head. "No, but I'm going to see him this afternoon."

"Would you mind if I tagged along? I'd like to find out more."

"I don't mind at all. It'll be nice to have some company." We made arrangements for her to pick me up around three at the barn.

"What do you think that's all about?" Marguerite asked.

"I don't know. But there's a reason someone wants to buy these properties and I mean to find out what it is."

* * *

Renee picked me up at the barn promptly at three. I took a few minutes to show her what had been accomplished so far, then we headed to her father's house. Five minutes later we parked in front of a small farmhouse. We went inside and Renee introduced me to her dad.

"Nice to meet you," Darrell Freeman said, shaking my hand.

Mr. Freeman was either older than I imagined or had aged due to illness. Renee was close to my age, so I figured her father would be in his fifties or early sixties. His hair was white and he was thin and frail.

"Dad, I brought Kate with me to look at the papers your lawyer gave you."

Mr. Freeman looked at me. "Are you some kind of legal expert? Not that I don't trust lawyers or anything."

"I'm definitely not," I said. "I'm just interested in the offer you received for your property. I learned there's someone who wants to buy mine as well. I inherited Stan Parker's orchard."

"So you're the one opening up a brewery," he said.

"It's a cidery, Dad. Not a brewery," Renee said. "Kate makes hard apple cider."

"Sounds tasty. When can I try some?" he asked.

I told him I just started a batch but he could be the first to try it. Mr. Freeman offered me coffee but I declined. We sat at his kitchen table and he slid a folder over to Renee.

"Here's the stuff the lawyer dropped off."

Renee opened the folder and flipped through the contents. "I thought you said there was an offer for the farm in here."

"I didn't say it was in here," Mr. Freeman said. "I said the lawyer told me someone wanted to buy the place."

"Do you know who?" I asked.

"Nope," he said. "And I don't care. Renee is going to get the farm. When I'm gone she can do what she wants with it. Besides, where would I go if I sell? I'm too old to move anywhere."

"Robert didn't give you any idea who it was?" Renee asked.

"Robert?" I said. "Robert Larabee?"

Mr. Freeman nodded. "Do you know him?"

I explained that he was the attorney who handled my uncle's estate and he had been the one who told me someone wanted to buy the orchard.

"I don't like this," Renee said, "especially if the same person is looking to buy both properties."

"I agree," I said. Something wasn't right. "Why would someone want all this land? I doubt they'd want to keep the farms and orchards going. Maybe they want to develop the area?"

"Maybe," Renee said. "But we're a small town. There's no reason to build a bunch of houses. There isn't much in the way of business—people would have really long commutes to get to work. The Morrison plant is about the only thing around here."

I thought of something. "Robert's law firm is in a mostly empty office park. There's lots of room for expansion."

"There still wouldn't be enough in the way of jobs," Renee said.

"Have you heard anything about some kind of factory wanting to move here?" I asked.

Renee shook her head. "And as fast as news spreads around here, everyone would know about it if that was the case."

Mr. Freeman reached for the folder and closed it. "Well, I'm not selling. I'm not going anywhere until the good Lord sees fit to take me home. That lawyer can go jump in the lake."

* * *

After Renee dropped me off at the barn, I checked the gauge on the fermentation tank to make sure everything was as it should be, then went home. It was a little early for dinner, but I was hungry and so was Blossom. She made it clear in no uncertain terms that her food dish was empty.

"Sorry, kitty," I said as I scooped kibble into her dish. I think she forgave me because she rubbed against my leg before digging in.

I didn't feel like cooking, so after I made a sandwich, I opened the bottle of pinot grigio I put in the refrigerator the other day, and poured some into a juice glass. While I ate I thought about the offers on the orchard and the other adjoining properties.

Daniel had taken the bank statements with him, but the topographic map was still on the table. I pushed my plate to the side and opened it in front of me. There were nine farms or orchards marked on the map. Three had been sold, and offers had been made on at least two that I knew of—mine and Renee's dad's. Daniel said he hadn't received any kind of offer and I wondered about the other four properties. That would be something to look into. I didn't believe it was a coincidence that Mr. Freeman and I had the same attorney. I wondered who had handled the parcels that had been sold and who they'd been sold to.

I retrieved my laptop from the living room and opened the web browser. Within a minute I was on the Adams County real estate site. Thompson was the only property owner's name I knew, so I typed that in. The search found way too many Thompsons and I had no way to narrow it down. I needed addresses or parcel numbers. And I needed to talk to Robert.

I looked at the clock on the stove. It was six o'clock, but he could still be at his office. I pressed his number on my phone.

"Larabee Law Office," Cindy Larabee said. "How may I help you?"

"Hi, Cindy. This is Kate Mulligan. Is Robert available?"

"I'm sorry," she said. "He's out of town for a few days. He had a meeting in Harrisburg. Is it important?"

"I just had some questions about something that came up."

"Could Mr. Bradford help?"

I'd almost forgotten Robert had a partner now. "Possibly. But I could wait until Robert gets back."

"Nonsense. Ian has an opening tomorrow at ten if you'd like to come in."

I knew it could wait, but I wasn't going to turn down the chance to get my questions answered. Part of me wondered if I was on a wild goose chase but, if nothing else, I'd learn who wanted these properties. I felt in my gut that the map I'd found at Carl's must be connected—I just didn't know how. And if it was all linked to his murder, I needed to know.

I'd just washed the dishes when there was a knock on the front door. I quickly dried my hands and moved to answer it. Through the window I saw Daniel.

"Sorry to bother you," he said when I let him in, "but I wanted you to know that I stopped in to see Scott today."

I showed him into the living room. "Can I get you something to drink?"

"No thanks," he said.

"Did you have dinner? I could fix you a sandwich."

"I actually had one of those frozen meals from Carl's freezer." He made a face. "You did the right thing passing them up. It was barely edible. Thanks anyway, though."

We sat down. "What did Scott have to say?" I asked.

"He was appreciative that you turned the statements over to him," Daniel said.

"That's it?"

"He's going to subpoena the rest of Carl's financial records to see if anything else pops." Daniel paused. "He has a theory."

"About Carl's murder?"

Daniel shook his head. "About the recent deposits. I'm not sure I agree with him just yet. I got to know Carl over the past few years, and I always thought he was a straight-up kind of guy. Sort of what you see is what you get."

I wasn't sure where this was going. "What's his theory?"

"Scott thinks Carl was blackmailing someone."

"What? That's ridiculous. Who? There has to be another explanation."

"That's what I told him," Daniel said. "Carl was nothing but honest with me, and especially with Stan. He never took a dime from Stan that wasn't owed him."

"Scott has to be wrong. Besides, who around here would he even blackmail? It doesn't make sense."

"It doesn't," Daniel said. "But the money came from somewhere. Scott will know more once he gets the rest of Carl's financials and talks to the bank. If the deposits were checks, that will show who wrote them. If they were cash, well . . ."

I had a thought. "Would a blackmailer really deposit the money into their bank account? That's kind of stupid. I sure wouldn't if I were swindling someone."

Daniel grinned. "Somehow I can't picture you blackmailing anyone. You'd probably confess if you even thought of doing it."

"And how would you know what I'd do? Maybe I'm a master criminal."

"You sound insulted that I think you have integrity."

"I'm not. Not really, anyway. Let's get back on track."

We tossed a few ideas back and forth without coming to any kind of conclusion. We'd have to wait until Scott uncovered something. I told Daniel about my visit with Renee's father and about the offer he'd received. "I don't think it's a coincidence that Mr. Freeman's attorney is Robert Larabee and he mentioned a potential buyer to both of us. I'm wondering if the others were also Robert's clients."

"Have you talked to Larabee?" Daniel asked.

"He's out of town for a couple of days but I have an appointment to see his partner, Ian Bradford, tomorrow."

"I don't think I've met him. Want some company?"

"Why?"

Daniel shrugged. "I know Larabee a little from helping Stan with a few things. I think I should meet his partner. Besides, I feel kind of left out that no one has said they want to buy my orchard."

I arranged to pick him up at nine fifteen. After he left, I found a mystery movie on TV and watched until I got sleepy. Then I went upstairs, got ready for bed, and was asleep in minutes.

* * *

At precisely ten in the morning, Cindy Larabee walked us to Ian Bradford's office. Where Robert's office was what I envisioned of an old school law firm, with dark polished wood, Ian Bradford's was ultra-modern. Chrome and glass were dominant. The walls were painted a stark white with chrome-framed black-and-white artwork on the walls. Definitely not to my taste.

Ian got up from his desk to shake my hand as I came through the doorway, followed by Daniel. He seemed surprised but recovered quickly.

"Welcome," Ian said. "I didn't realize you'd be bringing a friend."

"I hope you don't mind." I introduced Daniel.

"Not at all." Ian invited us to sit and went back around his desk. "Cindy tells me you have some questions I might be able to answer since Robert is away."

"I'm just wondering about the offer for my orchard that Robert mentioned."

"So you're considering it? That's great." He looked at Daniel. "Let me guess. You talked her into it?"

"I'm sure Kate is capable of making up her own mind," Daniel said.

Ian stared at Daniel for a moment. "Do I know you from somewhere? I get the feeling we've met before."

Daniel shook his head. "I doubt it. I've lived in Orchardville for years. You're new to the area, aren't you?"

"I moved here from Harrisburg eight months ago." Ian looked back at me. "Let me get all your information to pass on to Robert so he can get this moving."

"I didn't say I wanted to accept the offer," I said. "I only want to know more about it, so I can make an informed decision. It's not something I want to take lightly."

"Of course not," Ian said. "I'm not sure how much I can tell you. Robert takes care of the individual clients. I mostly handle our corporate clients. What do you need to know?"

On the drive over, Daniel and I had talked about how much to tell Ian. We decided to let him think I was considering selling the orchard. He'd be willing to give us more information if I didn't just blurt out that we knew about the other offers and sales. I was a little reluctant, but he also suggested making it seem like Robert had mentioned the offers.

I mentally crossed my fingers behind my back. I didn't like telling half-truths. I'd never been very good at it. "When Robert stopped to see me a few days ago, he mentioned the buyer—he told me, but I forget who—had bought some other properties near mine. I'm wondering if you could give me those names so I can talk to them."

"I'm sorry. I don't have that information," Ian said. "Like I told you, Robert is the one handling that."

"Can't you check his files? Or have Cindy look?"

"Not without Robert's permission. He should be back in town in another day or so and you can ask him yourself."

Daniel spoke up. "Wouldn't any sales be public record? You should be able to access that information."

"I'd need something to go on," Ian said. "And I don't have anything." He stood. "I'll tell Robert you stopped in and let him know you want to talk about selling your place."

I didn't correct him. We stood as well. "Thank you for your time," I said.

Cindy was making copies when we left Ian's office. "I hope Ian was able to help," she said.

"Unfortunately, no. He didn't have the information I wanted," I said. "Would you have Robert call me when he's available?"

"Of course."

"That was a waste of time," I said to Daniel when we were back in my SUV.

"Not necessarily."

"But he didn't know anything."

"He knew more than he was letting on," Daniel said. "For some reason he wasn't willing to say."

"How do you figure that?"

"Body language and the fact that he seemed willing to help when he thought you had decided to sell."

"Possibly." But now that I thought about it, Ian changed his tune right after he thought he had met Daniel before. "Was Ian correct that he'd met you before?"

"Why would you ask that?"

"You didn't deny it."

"I said I doubted we'd met, which is true."

"What about in Harrisburg? Isn't that where you lived before you moved here?"

"That was ten years ago," Daniel said. "Anyway, it's not important. Are you going back to the cider house? I don't have anything planned for the rest of the day. I can put together the framing for the bar. I just need to know what you have in mind."

Nice way to change the subject. He did it every time I tried to find out anything about him. I didn't understand why. My life was pretty much an open book. I was new here and everyone knew almost everything about me. Not so with Daniel. Was it that he didn't trust me? Or was he hiding something like Carl?

I accepted Daniel's offer to help. Levi was coming back to install the man door and he could help with that too, in addition to framing the bar. I was almost finished with putting the wood planks on the walls, and I'd continue with that.

While we worked that afternoon, I tried to figure out what Daniel could be hiding. Something had happened in his past before he came here. Good or bad, I meant to find out what it was.

Chapter Twelve

I put Carl's murder and everything else out of my mind for the rest of the day. Daniel framed the bar in record time and by late afternoon we had the corrugated metal around the front and sides. I marked where a row of cabinets and a triple sink for washing glasses would go. I left a message for Jack Riggs that the area was ready for plumbing. Levi had just finished installing the door, so I explained what I needed in the way of electric and showed him the refrigeration unit to be put in under the bar for the kegs. Levi and Jack worked well together, so I didn't envision any problems. I just needed my taps to arrive.

After everyone left for the day, I took a few pictures of the progress with my phone. I'd add them to the website and the Facebook page. Actually I'd have to do more than that. As soon as I had come up with the name Red Barn Cider Works, I bought the domain and I had a placeholder for the website, but that's about all I'd done. Some places only used their Facebook page, but I thought it was a better idea to have both. It would be a little more work, but if it got to be too much, I'd hire someone to handle it. I could post these to Facebook right away and now that the cidery was well on its way, I could start on the website. That had been one of my duties at the place I managed in Pittsburgh, which would really come in handy now.

When I got home, I took care of Blossom and tried to figure out what to make for dinner. I could have had another sandwich, but I wanted something more substantial. Unfortunately, that would involve defrosting something and cooking it. I decided to go out. I'd gotten used to eating alone in restaurants over the past few months, but it wasn't my favorite thing to do. I picked up my cell phone and pressed Marguerite's number.

"Want to get a bite to eat somewhere?" I asked when she answered.

"Funny you should ask," she said. "Noah and I were just talking about calling you to see if you wanted to join us."

"I guess great minds really do think alike. I don't want to butt in, though."

"Don't be silly. There's a great place just outside of town. It's kind of a dive, but they have good food."

Marguerite said she and Noah would pick me up in about forty-five minutes. That would give me just enough time to clean up and change out of the grubby clothes I'd worked in all day. After a quick shower, I half dried my hair and put on some fresh jeans and a shirt. I still had a few minutes so I flicked on some mascara and dabbed on a little blush. My friends arrived right on time.

Twenty minutes later Noah pulled his vintage Mustang into the parking lot of the Sunset Inn. The back seat was a little cramped. My legs were stiff when I got out and I tried not to limp, but Marguerite noticed.

"Are you all right?" she asked.

"I'm fine. I'm just a little stiff."

"I should have let you sit in the front."

"I'm fine," I said. "I've been overdoing it a bit, that's all."

"Are you sure?" Noah said.

I assured them I was okay and we went inside. The Sunset Inn wasn't as much of a dive as I'd imagined. I'd seen much worse in

Pittsburgh—especially when I was a student at Pitt. The place was old and probably hadn't been remodeled for years. The décor just about screamed eighties. It was reasonably clean, though, which was a plus.

On the ride over, I had learned that it was Noah's favorite restaurant and it was owned by one of his cousins. Apparently everyone who worked there knew him. The hostess, whose name tag read Taffy, showed us to a dark, wood-clad booth. Noah slid in beside Marguerite, and I took the bench across from them.

"What do you think?" Noah asked.

"I'm keeping an open mind. Did I read the hostess's name tag right? Her name is Taffy?"

"Yeah," Noah said. "She's my cousin. My aunt loved Ocean City so she named her after her favorite candy."

"Seriously?" I said.

"It's a good thing she's an only child," Marguerite said. "Her siblings would be named Salt and Water."

Noah laughed "Hey, these are my relatives you're talking about."

A server came by and we ordered drinks. Besides the usual burgers and appetizers, the menu listed a lot of comfort foods like meat loaf and fried chicken. I asked Noah how the chicken was and he guaranteed it was the best around. I ordered the chicken, mashed potatoes, and green beans with bacon vinaigrette.

"So what happened with Renee yesterday?" Marguerite asked. "Did you talk to her dad?"

I filled them in about the visit and about Daniel and I going to see Ian Bradford. I also mentioned how he thought he had met Daniel before. "He seemed willing to help until then. Daniel said he didn't think they'd ever met, but I'm not so sure."

"Why not?" Marguerite asked.

"For one thing, they both came from Harrisburg."

"Yeah," Noah said, "but Daniel's been here for what? Ten years or more? A lot of people live in Harrisburg."

"I know that," I said. "What bugs me is that when I asked Daniel about it, he changed the subject right away. He does that every time I ask him anything about himself."

Noah and Marguerite exchanged glances.

There was something they weren't telling me. "What?"

"Nothing," Marguerite said.

"Don't give me that. You two know something."

"It's not my decision," Marguerite said. "When Daniel wants you to know, he'll tell you. In the meantime, just know that you can trust him."

"So I'm supposed to trust him, but apparently he doesn't trust me enough to tell me whatever it is he's hiding."

Marguerite reached across the table and put her hand on mine. "He doesn't want to burden you."

This was so frustrating. Everyone in Orchardville probably knew whatever it was except me. "Burden me with what? What did he do? Kill someone?"

"Nothing like that," Noah said.

"He knows you've been through a lot in the past year. Let's talk about something else," Marguerite said. "How's the work at the cidery going?"

I'd go along with changing the subject for now, but the issue with Daniel wasn't going away. He was going to talk to me and answer my questions. I'd make sure of it. I told my friends about the progress at the barn.

"That's great," Marguerite said. "I have a surprise for you. Kind of, anyway."

"Really? I remember some of your surprises when we were kids. Should I be scared?"

Noah laughed. "I've heard about some of those. This one is good. I promise."

"For a while now," Marguerite said, "I've been wanting to expand. I have enough employees at the café to cover when I'm not there."

"So you're retiring?" I knew that would never happen.

"Let me finish. I bought a food truck."

This was definitely a surprise. "Why?"

"Stop interrupting! It'll be a great way to pick up new customers, and some outside of Orchardville. I've already got a few weekends booked and I thought—if it's okay with you—that I'd bring it for your opening."

"I would love that," I said. "Aren't you overextending yourself, though? The café is pretty busy."

"It is, but like I said, I have enough staff to cover. If I have to hire a few more people, I will. I'll keep the food truck weekends only, and only for a few hours at first." She smiled. "Except for your opening. I'll be there for the duration or until I run out of food, whichever comes first."

I was excited for her. "So tell me about this truck."

"It's only a few years old and it's in great shape. It's also fully equipped, which is a big plus," she said. "All it needs is a new paint job with the name and logo."

"Have you decided on a name?" I asked.

"Well, everyone in town knows Margie's Morsels, so I'm calling it *Margie's Morsels On the Go.*"

"I love it," I said. "It's the perfect name. Your mom would be really proud of you."

"I think so," Marguerite said.

We talked more about her new venture while we ate. Afterward, we were debating whether we had room for dessert when Noah nudged Marguerite. "Don't look now," he said, "but Cherry Perry just came in."

Marguerite groaned.

"Cherry Perry?" I turned around to see. A fiftyish woman with rainbow-striped hair stood by the front register. She wore bright blue capris and a hot pink short-sleeved blouse. That was a lot of color, but she looked harmless to me. "That's really her name? Who is she?"

"I really hope she doesn't spot us." Marguerite looked at me. "Cherry owns CertainTea, the tea shop in town. "She will talk your ear off."

Noah said, "She's a nice lady, she just doesn't know when to stop—uh-oh. She's coming this way."

"Marguerite! Noah! How nice to see you! And who is this? You must be the new girl in town."

I introduced myself. Without being asked, she slid in beside me.

"I'm Cherry," she said. "You must stop in and try one of my teas. I blend them all myself. I have all kinds—traditional, herbal, medicinal, you name it."

"I'll do that," I said when she finally took a breath.

Cherry touched my arm. "I am so sorry about Carl. He was a wonderful man. So kind, so caring. It's just awful. I don't know what this world is coming to. To have someone in our little town murdered! And the police don't know why. I asked Chief Flowers about it. I told him he should call in the FBI. Maybe those *Criminal Minds* people, like they have on TV. What if there's a serial killer running loose? No one's safe."

It took all my willpower not to laugh.

"Uh," Marguerite said. "It wasn't a serial killer."

"You don't know that," Cherry said. "He could just be getting started."

I wondered what kind of medicinal tea she blended and how much of it she drank.

"That doesn't make sense," Marguerite said. "Do you know what serial means?"

"Of course I do," Cherry said. "We'd all better be careful is all I'm saying."

"How well did you know Carl?" I asked.

"Well enough, I suppose. We went out on a date once. Maybe not exactly a date. I got stood up on another date and he bought me a drink and drove me home. Does that count as a date? I think it does even though he didn't try to kiss me or anything. Just told me to take care. He was a nice man, even though not everyone thought so."

Cherry paused to take a breath so I said, "Who didn't like him?"

"Let me think. Will Pearson for one. Have you met him?"

I was about to say I had, but she didn't stop talking.

"He owns the collectibles store. Eli Jennings is another."

"Renee's husband?" I said.

"Yes," Cherry answered. "Some others I can't think of right now. There was a man in a suit that I saw him talking to a couple of times. Come to think of it, the last time I saw them in town they were arguing and about to engage in fisticuffs."

That was the first time I'd ever heard the word fisticuffs used in conversation. "Who was it?" I asked. "Who was Carl fighting with?"

Cherry shrugged. "Darned if I know."

"Well, what did he look like?" Marguerite asked.

"He looked sort of ordinary, except for the suit," Cherry said. "And the funny looking tie. He looked like one of those rich oil men you see on TV."

There was only one person I knew who fit that description. Robert Larabee.

"What were they arguing about?" I asked Cherry.

"Darned if I know," she said. "I was fixing a teapot display in the window and they were across the street in front of The Tavern. Carl looked like he was yelling, so someone might have heard them. The guy in the funny suit grabbed Carl's arm and Carl pulled it away and yelled some more. Then the suit guy walked away."

"When did this happen?" Noah asked.

"I don't know. Maybe a couple weeks ago? I remember it was nice out that day and it rained the day before. I remember that because I was mad that it rained because I'd just cleaned the window and I had to do it over again the next day before I did my window display. Just think, if I'd cleaned the window fifteen minutes later, I would have heard the argument."

An argument on a public street, especially when the weather was nice, must have been witnessed by someone. "About what time of day was the argument?"

"Late morning, I think," Cherry said.

"So, around ten or eleven?" I asked.

"Yeah, probably around then."

I made eye contact with Marguerite and tilted my head toward the door hoping she'd get the message that I wanted to leave. When the waitress stopped to see if we wanted dessert, Noah asked for the check. She handed it to him and he passed her his credit card. He refused when I offered to pay my share.

Cherry turned to me. "It was lovely meeting you. Be sure to stop in and try some of my tea." She stood. "I really hope they catch that killer before he strikes again." She turned, waved to someone sitting at the bar, and headed that way.

"Whew," I said.

"What do you think about what she told you about Carl?" Marguerite said. "I wonder who he was arguing with."

"I know exactly who. Unless someone else dresses like a Texas oil man, it was my attorney, Robert Larabee."

"I've never actually met him," Marguerite said. "What do you think they were arguing about?"

"My guess is it was about Robert wanting me to sell the orchard. They definitely didn't see eye to eye on that. And now that I know one of Robert's clients was after some other properties as well, I wonder if Carl knew about them. Maybe Robert was paying Carl to keep it to himself."

"Why would he do that?" Noah asked.

"I don't know." We got up to leave.

"Maybe Carl was blackmailing Robert," Marguerite said.

It was the same theory Daniel had told me that Scott had come up with. "I hate to think that Carl would do that," I said. "But the money came from somewhere. And if Robert was paying him for his silence and Carl threatened to expose Robert and his buyer, then Robert could have silenced him permanently."

Chapter Thirteen

It was almost ten when Noah and Marguerite dropped me off. Blossom voiced her displeasure that her food dish was half empty, so I topped it off for her and gave her a few treats. I couldn't stop thinking about Carl and Robert. I needed to tell Scott Flowers about it so he could interview Cherry. I doubted that he already had or I'm sure Cherry would have mentioned it. She sure talked about everything else.

I hated thinking that Robert could be a murderer, but it made more sense than anything else I'd considered. It also made sense that the money Carl had received came from Robert. What I didn't get, though, was why Robert had been paying him. If the property offers and the sales that had taken place so far were on the up and up, there was no reason for Carl to extort money from Robert. There had to be something else going on. And there had to be a big reason why someone wanted this land. I needed to find out what it was, but I had no idea how. I was too tired to figure it out tonight. I put it aside for the moment and headed to bed.

* * *

The next morning, I met Jack and Levi at the barn. While they worked on the electric and plumbing for the bar area, I finished installing the rest of the wood on the last wall and around the door that Levi had put in the day before. I got a nice surprise before noon when the furniture for the cidery arrived a few days early. I put two tables and a few chairs out, but I wouldn't place most of it until I did the final cleaning. It would definitely be nice to have a place to sit. By lunchtime, Jack and Levi had the wiring and plumbing finished. All that was left was hooking up the refrigeration unit and installing the sinks. When Jack and Levi left for lunch, I retrieved the peanut butter sandwich I'd packed and sat down at a table with my laptop.

I logged on and headed to Google. I typed in Robert Larabee. The usual stuff came up, mostly about his law firm. I scrolled through several pages. If he was hiding something, he was doing a good job of it. Entering Carl's name didn't turn up anything at all. There were a lot of Carl Randolphs, but none in this area.

I tried a different tactic. I typed in *recent real estate sales near Orchardville, PA*. The top two entries were for two popular real estate websites. I practically kicked myself for not thinking to check these earlier. I selected the first one, and the site even had a handy map with all the sales. It was easy to find the properties on the map. I didn't have a notebook with me, but I took a pen from my purse and picked up a scrap piece of cardboard to jot down some notes.

I found the Thompson farm with no trouble. This site didn't show the sellers or the buyers, but it gave me an address that I could enter in the county site and get all the information I needed. Ten minutes later I had what I needed for the surrounding properties. I was just about to go to the county site when Daniel came in.

"Sitting down on the job, I see," he said.

I smiled. "That's one of the perks of being the owner."

"Nice furniture, by the way. Are you working on something or just goofing off?" He pulled out a chair and sat down.

I told him what I'd found just now and filled him in on my conversation with Cherry Perry.

"You have to take what she told you with a grain of salt," Daniel said. "She looks for conspiracies everywhere."

"I figured that, what with her comment about it being a serial killer, but Scott still needs to know about the argument between Robert and Carl."

"Agreed. When is Larabee due back?"

"I'm not sure. Maybe tomorrow? I'll find out. In the meantime, I'm going to see who bought these properties and go into town and see if anyone else saw the fight."

"I'll go with you."

"You don't have to do that. I'm sure you have better things to do."

"Frankly, there's not much to do with the orchard at the moment as long as we don't expect a freeze. Then I'll get a little busy."

I hadn't considered that. Truthfully, I hadn't thought about the orchard at all. I had relied on Carl before, and since his death the acres of trees had been far from my mind. I had no idea what I'd have to do, and now I didn't have a manager to take care of it. I was going to have to hire someone, and quick. I sighed.

"What is it?"

"My orchard," I said. "I don't know anything about managing it."

"I'm happy to help when I can," he said.

"I appreciate that, but you have your own trees to deal with. I need to hire someone and I don't even know where to start."

"I can definitely help with that. There are a couple of guys—twin brothers—who worked here last summer and were hoping to hire on somewhere full time this year. They're not Carl, but they know orchards. Between the two of them they should be able to handle it. Do you speak Spanish?"

"Not a word," I said. "I took French in school and can only remember a few words of it."

"These guys are graduating next month from the local community college. Their parents immigrated here from Mexico before they were born and they speak fluent Spanish. Most of the seasonals that come here every year are from Mexico, so that would be a definite plus."

"They're kind of young. Don't I want someone with more experience?"

"Their age isn't an issue. I've seen them work. They studied horticulture and they've worked the orchards around here, including mine, ever since they were old enough."

I still wasn't convinced. "I'm not sure I can afford to hire both of them. I'd want to pay each of them at least what Carl was making."

"You're going to need people to work here at the cidery too, aren't you?"

"I will once I'm established."

"Which won't be long," Daniel said. "You're going to do a booming business. At least talk to them and then decide."

I agreed to at least do that much. Daniel gave me their names—Greg and Gary Diaz. He'd have them stop in to see me in a day or two. I still wasn't sure, but I needed someone to help with the orchard. I only hoped it worked out.

Jack and Levi returned from lunch then. Daniel and I helped them move the refrigeration unit into place. This would hold the kegged cider with taps above for serving. It was only then I remembered I still needed to buy an actual refrigerator with an ice maker. Thank goodness I'd saved a spot for one under the bar. I double checked the measurements and went back to my laptop and ordered one before I forgot again.

While Daniel helped Jack and Levi, I opened the county site and clicked the link for the page I needed. This site was a little different than the one in Allegheny County that I'd used in the past. It opened to a map of Adams County with a block near the top to enter the address. I typed in the address of the Thompson farm. I found the listing easily. It showed the location on the map, the assessed value, the date sold, and the owner's name.

The new owner was listed as MMC, LLC. A company of some sort with a post office box for an address. I opened a new tab and googled the name. Nothing at all came up. So who, or rather what, was MMC? I checked the next property on my list and it had also been purchased by MMC. I called Daniel over to take a look.

"Have you ever heard of this company—MMC?" I asked.

"No, I haven't."

Jack came over to the table. "Did I hear you say MMC?"

"Yes," I said. "Are you familiar with it?"

"I am now," Jack said. "I own two acres next to the old Thompson farm, and MMC is buying them. I don't have any use for the land—I like living in town—so I'm unloading it. The closing is next week."

"What is MMC?" Daniel asked. "What do they do? Who owns it?"

"I have no idea. All I know is they made an offer for way more than the land is worth and I accepted." He looked at me. "The only person I've met with is that lawyer of yours—Larabee."

Somehow I wasn't surprised. "It looks like this MMC also bought the Thompson farm and a couple other properties. Do you know what they plan to do with that land?"

Jack shook his head. "Nope. Don't take this the wrong way, but they can do whatever they want with it. Doesn't matter to me. Carl thought I was an idiot for selling, but I made out good. I'm buying a new Harley and paying off a few bills with the proceeds."

"Carl thought you shouldn't sell?" I said.

"Yep. He thought I'd regret it. It wasn't any of his business, and I told him that more than once."

That must have been what he and Carl had been arguing about outside the barn. I remembered Carl telling him he'd regret it. I also remembered Jack's response. "Why did Carl think you'd regret it?"

"He wouldn't say. Said he couldn't tell me more than it was a bad decision."

After Jack went back to work, I looked at Daniel. "What in the world is going on?"

"Damned if I know."

I pulled out my phone. "I'm calling Robert. He's the only one who knows what this is all about."

Cindy Larabee answered as usual. I told her I needed to speak with Robert. She informed me he would be back in the office the following day. I considered waiting until then, but I wanted answers. After some back and forth, she gave me his cell phone number. I called and got his voice mail. I asked him to call me immediately, that it was important.

"Now what?" I said more to myself than to Daniel, but he answered anyway.

"That's all we can do with this information for now. Why don't we go into town and see if anyone witnessed the argument between Carl and Larabee?"

I agreed. Jack and Levi were finishing up for the day, so we waited until they left and I locked up. Even if nothing came of our questions, I'd get dinner at The Tavern when we were done. It would be one more day I didn't have to cook.

* * *

We headed to town in Daniel's truck and parked in front of Scent-Sations. Last night Cherry had mentioned that Renee's husband, Eli, hadn't liked Carl. I decided to pay a visit to see if Eli was there while Daniel stopped to see Will Pearson. As luck would have it, Eli was at the counter when I entered the store.

Eli Jennings looked like he could be a defenseman for the Pittsburgh Steelers. His muscular arms were bigger than some women's waists. He was probably older than Renee by a good ten years, and his curly black hair was beginning to gray at the temples. He smiled as the door closed behind me. "Let me guess," he said, "you're Kate."

I returned his smile. "Correct. How did you guess?"

"Honestly, it wasn't much of a guess. Renee told me all about you. We appreciate the business."

"I love what she's planning for the cidery. Is Renee here?"

Eli shook his head. "Her father had a doctor's appointment today and she takes him anywhere he needs to go."

"You're actually the one I wanted to talk to anyway."

He gave me a puzzled look.

"It's about Carl Randolph," I said.

"What about him?"

Now that I was here, I wasn't sure what to ask. I didn't want to come right out and say what Cherry had alluded to. "I'm sure you know by now that Carl passed away."

Eli nodded. "I do. I was so sorry to hear that. Carl was a great guy."

That was the complete opposite of what Cherry told me. "So you were friends?"

"Sort of," he said. "I volunteer with a group of troubled kids, and we showed them around Stan's orchard a few times. It's amazing what getting out in nature will do for kids. Carl was great with them—really patient answering their questions. Every once in a while Carl and I would meet up for a beer over at The Tavern. Why did you want to know if we were friends?"

After what he told me, there was no way I was bringing up Cherry's remark. I said the first thing that popped into my mind. "I'm thinking of having a wake for Carl sometime next week. I'm hoping you and Renee will be able to make it."

He assured me they would, and I said I'd let them know the exact date. I sighed as I stepped out onto the sidewalk. I guess I now had a wake to plan. And a funeral, now that I thought about it. I still had no idea what Carl's final wishes had been. He had no family to make a decision, so it was up to me. I'd have to contact a local funeral director and see what the options were.

Daniel joined me minutes later and we compared notes. Will Pearson told him he hadn't seen Carl have any kind of argument with anyone in the past few weeks. I was beginning to wonder if Cherry had imagined the whole thing. If it hadn't been for the fact that Robert was instrumental in making offers to buy properties for MMC I'd let the whole thing drop. But I wasn't ready to do that yet.

We were walking into The Tavern when Scott pulled up in his squad car. "Got a minute?" he asked. I wasn't sure which one of us he was talking to, but we both turned and walked to his car as he got out. "Kate, have you heard from Robert Larabee in the last couple of days?"

"Robert Larabee?"

"He's the attorney who handled your uncle's estate, isn't he?" Scott asked.

"Yes, he is. Actually, I've been trying to get hold of him with no luck. He's out of town and is supposed to be back tomorrow. Have you talked to his wife?"

"What's going on, Scott?" Daniel asked.

"His wife called me thirty minutes ago and reported him missing."

Chapter Fourteen

"Missing?" I said. "I just talked to Cindy Larabee a couple of hours ago and she never mentioned that. She told me he'd be back tomorrow and gave me his cell phone number."

"Apparently she's been worried that he hasn't answered his phone or returned her calls," Scott said.

"She never let on when I spoke to her."

"It gets worse," Scott said. "She finally called the hotel where he was registered and he never checked in. No one has seen him."

Daniel and I shared a glance.

"You two know something, don't you?" Scott said.

Daniel spoke up. "Not about him being missing. And none of it makes much sense."

Scott looked at his watch. "I'm off the clock as of right now—"

"When are you ever off the clock?" Daniel asked.

"Some of us don't get to leave the job."

Daniel said, "Some of us didn't have a choice."

"You had a choice."

"Not a good one," Daniel said.

I kept looking back and forth between the two. What did all that mean?

"Anyway, I'm hungry," Scott said. "How about we go inside and you can fill me in."

The Tavern was nearly empty and we were told to sit anywhere, so we took a booth in a corner. After placing our orders, Scott said, "So, what do you know that I don't?"

I told him what Cherry Perry had said about Robert and Carl arguing but that so far we couldn't verify it.

"And you probably won't be able to," Scott said. "She calls at least once a day with her theories on who killed Randolph. I'll ask around, though, in case she's right for a change. I doubt she is, though."

Daniel and I both told him what we'd discovered about the property sales and offers and Robert's involvement with the mysterious buyer. Scott agreed that the money paid to Carl had something to do with it.

"The money deposited to Randolph's account had been in cash," Scott said. "He must have discovered something about those sales and was blackmailing Larabee."

I shook my head. "I don't want to believe that Carl was a blackmailer. Maybe it was more like hush money. Someone paid him to keep quiet."

"What's the difference?" Scott asked. "If something illegal was going on, he should have reported it and not taken a payoff."

"We don't know that it was anything illegal," I said.

Scott actually rolled his eyes. "What else could it be?"

I didn't have an answer for that.

"I don't want to believe it either, but Scott may be right," Daniel said. "I liked Carl, but people do funny things when money's involved."

I hated to admit that either one of them might be right. The fact was that I had only seen one side of Carl. I didn't really know him. I hated the idea that he could have been a blackmailer, but I had to consider it. "What's our next step?" I asked.

"*Our?*" Scott said. "There's no *our* in this. *My* next step is to find Robert Larabee."

The server brought our burgers and talk stopped, but not for long. After a few bites, I put my burger down. "I have a theory," I said.

"Really." Scott didn't sound surprised. At least he didn't roll his eyes again. "I can't wait."

"You don't have to sound so sarcastic," I said. "I can keep it to myself."

He sighed. "Let's hear it."

"I think Robert is on the run. He stopped at the cidery a few days ago and told me again that he had a potential buyer for the orchard. I told him in no uncertain terms that it was never going to happen. He didn't press the point and left. But now I'm wondering if maybe someone at that MMC place threatened him somehow."

"That sounds possible," Daniel said.

I had more. "I also think Robert is the one who killed Carl. Either Robert refused to give Carl any more money and they fought, or Carl told him he wasn't going to keep his secret anymore. Robert grabbed the first thing available and hit Carl with it."

Scott was quiet for half a minute. "That's a good theory. It makes sense."

"I think I need that in writing," I said.

"Don't press your luck." Scott popped his last French fry into his mouth and pushed his plate aside. "I'm going to talk to Mrs. Larabee again and get some more information."

The server came with our check and Daniel grabbed it before I could. He looked at Scott. "I know you don't have to, but will you keep us in the loop?"

"If you do the same."

Daniel paid the bill and the three of us walked out together. Scott waved goodbye as he drove away. Daniel dropped me off at the barn, where I retrieved my laptop. I took a leisurely walk back to the house wondering if Cindy Larabee was as much in the dark as she'd let on to Scott. Surely she'd have known if her husband was making payouts to someone, either from the business account or their joint account. Unless they didn't have a joint account. Some couples liked to keep their funds separate. The more I thought about everything I'd learned so far, the more confused I got.

As hard as it was, I put all those thoughts aside when I got home. Blossom and I spent the rest of the evening parked on the couch watching TV. Tomorrow would be soon enough to exercise my brain again.

* * *

I was up early and, after taking care of Blossom, I headed into town to Margie's Morsels. I wanted to tell Marguerite the latest and ask if she knew a funeral director. The café had just opened for the day and there were no other customers. The aroma of freshly ground coffee beans smelled heavenly. Marguerite and Noah were behind the counter and separated from what appeared to be a pretty intense kiss when they heard the door open.

"Hey, that's enough of that," I teased. "What will the customers think?"

Marguerite's cheeks were flushed. "It might be the only thrill some of them get for the week."

I laughed. "Carry on, then."

Noah said, "You're here early today. What can I get you?"

"Surprise me."

He grinned. "You might be sorry. I came up with a new concoction yesterday. The jury's still out."

Marguerite came around the counter and we took seats at a table. "What brings you in this early? Is something going on?"

"Maybe I just wanted to visit my friends and get some decent coffee."

She snorted. "Yeah, right. I can see on your face that you have news, so spill."

I told her about what Daniel and I had discovered regarding the property sales.

"I've never heard of MMC," she said.

"So far no one has."

Noah brought over a tall mug with foam on the top and sat down next to Marguerite. "Here you go."

I took a sip and made a face.

"That bad, huh?" Marguerite said.

I took another sip just to be polite and had the same reaction. I pushed it aside.

Noah sighed. "Back to the drawing board, I guess."

"What's in that thing?" I asked. My tongue was burning.

"Espresso, oat milk, white chocolate, cinnamon, nutmeg, cardamom, maple syrup, cayenne—"

I held up my hand. "Stop right there. You put all that in one drink?"

He nodded.

"First, that's way too many things," I said. "Second, cayenne does not belong in coffee. Ever."

Noah got up. "I was going to call it *The Kitchen Sink*."

"And that's exactly where it belongs," Marguerite said. "In the sink and down the drain."

"No more surprises," he said. "I'll bring you a plain, old, boring coffee."

I continued telling Marguerite about yesterday and what Scott had told us. "Cindy Larabee never let on to me that she hadn't been able to get in touch with Robert. I think he's on the run." I told her my theory.

"That makes a lot of sense."

"What makes sense?" Noah asked as he put a steaming cup of coffee down in front of me and took a seat.

I repeated what I'd told Marguerite.

"I don't know," Noah said. "He has a good reputation around here. He's my sister's attorney. I don't see someone like that killing someone and running off. If Carl was blackmailing him, why wouldn't Larabee just turn him in to the police?"

"They're all good points," I said. "Robert has to be hiding something regarding those sales. Something illegal, or something the buyer doesn't want anyone to know. And why isn't there any information on MMC?"

"There's a record somewhere," Noah said. "I'm sure some government agency knows all about it."

A couple of customers came in then and Noah got up to take care of them. Marguerite rose as well and I asked her to wait a minute. I told her my plans for Carl's wake since he didn't have anyone else, and she gave me the name of a local funeral director.

When I got to the barn, I checked the cider batch. Everything had been installed, and the next few weeks would only involve cleaning and decorating. I'd be able to do a soft opening as soon as the cider was ready—earlier than I'd planned. With nothing pressing to do at the moment, I headed back to the house.

* * *

I sat down at the kitchen table with a bowl of cereal and my laptop. I went to the county real estate site again, but after thirty minutes I hadn't learned anything new. I had no idea how to find information about MMC. I considered calling Robert's office, but they had enough to deal with at the moment. I closed the laptop.

I waited until nine, then called the funeral director Marguerite had suggested and made an appointment to meet with him that afternoon. I straightened up the house a bit, which took all of about ten minutes. I dug a book out of the box containing a half dozen that I hadn't donated before I moved. Ten pages in, I realized I hadn't absorbed a word. I was too restless to concentrate. I decided maybe a walk would help.

The last time I'd gone through the orchard had been with Carl, and I wished I remembered half of what he'd told me. I knew there were apple, pear, and peach trees, and I recalled that two of the varieties of apple were perfect for cider. The trees that were just beginning to form buds when I arrived in Orchardville were blooming now. In another week they'd probably be in full bloom. Once the cidery was running well, I made a vow to myself to learn more about owning an orchard.

As I crossed the peach orchard, I spotted Daniel walking my way with two young men. I'd almost forgotten I'd promised to talk to the Diaz twins about working for me. I could hear the three discussing something in Spanish. When they reached me Daniel made the introductions.

Greg and Gary Diaz were as close to identical as I'd ever seen. If it hadn't been for Gary's full beard, I wouldn't have been able to tell them apart. They were tall and slim and both wore faded jeans and flannel shirts.

"It's nice to meet you both," I said as I shook their hands. "Daniel told me all about you two."

Greg laughed. "Not everything, I hope."

"Yeah," Gary said. "We'd like to stay out of trouble."

I smiled. "It was all good. I understand you worked for Carl last summer."

"We did," Greg said. "We were sorry to hear about what happened to him."

"He was a good guy," Gary added.

They had parked at the cidery, so we walked that way and they took turns telling me about working for various orchards over summer breaks and about their studies at the local college. For as young as they were, I was impressed. It seemed they had inherited their work ethic from their parents. I didn't think I could go wrong hiring them.

I showed them around the cidery and then we sat at the table. They were both interested in the cider-making process and had more than a few questions as to how it went from fruit on the trees to carbonated in a keg.

"I hope you don't mind," Daniel said, "but I told them my idea that if you hire them they could split duties between here and the orchard."

I looked at both of them. "Would you be okay with that?"

"Definitely," they said in unison.

"Frankly, it would be the best job ever," Greg said.

We discussed salary and they seemed fine with what I was willing to pay.

They fist-bumped each other when I gave them the good news that they were hired.

"You won't regret it," Daniel said. "Although I might since they won't be working for me anymore."

We set a start date of mid-May, after graduation, and they hopped in their old Honda and sped away. I turned to Daniel. "I don't remember ever being that young and enthusiastic."

He laughed. "Me neither. I think they'll work out well."

"I hope so. Thanks for recommending them."

"Sure."

"And thanks for your help with everything."

"You don't need to thank me," Daniel said. "I'm happy to help. By the way, I talked to a buddy in Harrisburg and he's going to see what he can find out about Larabee."

"How's he going to do that? Isn't that up to the police?"

"He is police. State police," Daniel said. "Scott put out a BOLO but I want to stay in the loop."

"Scott will keep us in the loop, won't he?"

"Mostly, but . . ." He didn't finish what he was going to say.

"But what?"

"Do you need help with anything?" Daniel asked.

He changed the subject again. "Stop doing that."

"Doing what?"

"You know what," I said. "Every time I ask a question where you might have to reveal a little bit about yourself you change the subject."

"I don't."

"Yes, you do. You did it just now. I think you know me well enough by now that you can trust me. You can tell me whatever it is you're hiding."

"I do trust you," Scott said. "And I'm not hiding anything. I just don't like talking about myself."

I rolled my eyes. "Fine! Don't, then. Apparently it's all right for everyone else to know whatever it is, but not me."

"That's not it."

I raised my hands in frustration. "You know what? Forget it. I don't want to know." I turned and started walking toward the fermentation tanks. I heard Daniel sigh.

"I used to be a state cop. I was almost killed in the line of duty. My partner wasn't so lucky."

Chapter Fifteen

I stopped and turned back around. "I'm so sorry. But why wouldn't you tell me this before?"

Daniel pulled out a chair. "It's a long story. Have a seat."

I sat and he took the chair across the table from me.

"I didn't want to burden you, what with all you've been through," he said.

I remembered Marguerite saying the same thing. "It wouldn't have been a burden. I'm stronger than I look."

"I know that now. And maybe I should have told you, but it was easier not to. Like I said, I don't like talking about myself."

"I understand that, believe me. So what happened?" I asked.

"Ten years ago I was with the criminal investigations section of the state police in Harrisburg. My partner, Reed McCoy, and I were on a raid at a warehouse. It all went south and the short version is Reed and one other guy were killed and I ended up in the trauma unit with three gunshot wounds. The docs removed two of the bullets, but one is lodged a little close to my spine. They forced me to find a new career."

That must have been what he was referring to with Scott the other night. "That's horrible. But you're okay now?"

"I guess. The bullet hasn't moved, so the docs say it's not likely to after all this time."

"That's good," I said.

"I had a choice between sitting at a desk all day or taking a disability retirement. A desk job would have killed me, so I chose the latter. It wasn't the plan I'd had for myself, but it's worked out. So that's it. The whole story."

"How did you end up owning an orchard?" I asked.

"I knew I wanted to buy some land somewhere in this area. At first I thought maybe a small farm, but when I saw the orchard for sale, I knew that's what I wanted to do. I didn't know a whole lot about growing fruit when I bought it, but I learned along the way. That's enough about me for today."

"I'm glad you told me. I'm sorry I had to badger you to do it."

He smiled. "No, you're not."

I returned the smile. "You're right. I'm not." But I was definitely glad he'd opened up.

Daniel left shortly after that, and I locked up and went back to the house. I made some lunch and took a catnap with Blossom. An hour later, I met with the funeral director and together we decided the best choice was cremation. He'd arrange everything with the coroner and let me know when it was finished. I'd have to figure out what to do with Carl's ashes later on.

I was fine during the meeting but on the way home I lost it and had to pull over. I hadn't been able to make the arrangements when Brian died. I'd been in the trauma unit, and his mother had done everything. She had him buried next to his father. I knew that's what had needed to be done but I never got to say goodbye. I had missed all of that. I had missed seeing him one last time. I had missed being able to grieve properly. And now I cried for Brian, for Uncle Stan who I wished I had known better, and for Carl.

* * *

As I arrived at the barn the next morning, Daniel pulled up in his truck and rolled down his window. "I wanted you to know before word gets out that the state police found Robert Larabee in his vehicle in a ravine."

"Is he . . ."

Daniel nodded. "They're going to do an investigation, but it looks like he might have missed a curve and gone off the road."

I shivered. I couldn't help thinking about Brian. "That's horrible."

"Scott went to inform Larabee's wife." He paused. "That's one thing I don't miss about the job. I never got used to making notifications."

"Poor Cindy," I said. "I know what she'll be going through. I'll have to pay her a visit."

"Are you all right? I'm meeting back up with Scott in a bit, but he won't mind if I cancel."

"I'll be okay. You don't need to stay."

Daniel studied me as if trying to see whether or not that was true.

"Really," I said. "I'll be fine."

He reached out through the open window and squeezed my arm. "I'll keep you posted if I learn anything else."

"Thanks for letting me know."

He drove off and I went inside. I sank into a chair. I felt terrible for thinking Robert had run off. Instead, he'd been dead in his car for days. I hoped he hadn't suffered. I didn't want to imagine otherwise. I shook off those thoughts. I'd done enough crying the day before and I had work to do. I got up and checked the tanks, then decided to do some cleaning. If I got everything in shape, I'd have Carl's wake here on Wednesday.

An hour later, my phone rang. It was Marguerite.

"Oh my God," she said. "I just heard about Robert Larabee. I can't believe it."

Word traveled fast, as usual around here. "Daniel told me as soon as he found out."

"Are you okay?"

"I am," I said. "It's just a shock. Here I'd been thinking Robert left town and instead he was lying dead in his car. I almost feel guilty for thinking that."

"You have nothing to feel guilty about," Marguerite said. "He still could have been on the run. You don't know that he wasn't. And don't forget, he might have killed Carl."

"You're right, of course. It doesn't make it any easier, though. I'm going to visit Cindy Larabee later today if you'd like to go with me."

"Sure. Can we make if after I close? Jen had a dentist appointment so she left early today."

We decided I'd pick her up at four, then I got back to work. I had the place spotless by lunchtime. The tables and chairs were in place, the countertop on the bar as well as the sinks shined. I would still have to install the taps when they arrived in a few days. The bathroom needed a mirror and to have the paper towel holder hung up, but it was functional. All I needed was for the cider to finish. I headed back to the house to get something to eat and take a shower.

I had some time before I had to pick up Marguerite, so I decided to do some shopping. I'd start with the hardware store. I could pick up a bathroom mirror and talk to Mike Thompson at the same time. I had some questions about the sale of his parents' farm that maybe he could answer. Mike was helping a customer pick out some electrical supplies, so I browsed while I waited for him to finish. I found a mirror with a rustic wooden frame and placed it in my shopping cart. I also found a shelf that would work in the bathroom to hold extra supplies. By the time Mike was available, I had half a cart full of stuff.

Mike smiled when he saw my cart. "Didn't you buy enough the last time you were here? Not that I'm complaining."

"I only came in for a mirror and made the mistake of browsing," I said. "Do you have a minute?"

"Sure. What can I help you with?"

"When I was in before you mentioned your folks sold their farm."

"They did."

"This might sound strange, but I got an offer for my orchard, and it seems like someone wants to buy almost all the properties in that area. Have you heard anything about that?"

Mike shook his head. "I only know about my parents' place. I don't keep in touch with any of the old neighbors."

"When I got the offer, I did a little checking and found that a company called MMC is behind it all."

"I really wouldn't know," Mike said. "I vaguely remember my dad said the attorney handled everything at the closing and he never actually met whoever bought the place. Is there some kind of problem?"

I honestly wasn't sure what to tell him. "Not that I know of. I just don't know anything about the company."

"I can give my dad a call and have him contact you. Maybe he knows."

"That would be great." I gave him my phone number, checked out, and went to pick up Marguerite.

* * *

Out of curiosity, I drove by the Thompson farm on the way into town. I pulled over near the driveway to the house. There were weeds beginning to grow in the gravel, and the house appeared empty. There were no cars and no activity anywhere. MMC obviously had no intention of farming the land. It was a big contrast to Renee's father's farm on the other side of the road. Although Mr. Freeman wasn't well enough to work it himself, there was someone on a tractor tilling one of the fields. I drove on.

I kept asking myself why I cared for what reason the properties were being purchased, especially now that Robert was dead. Would his wife or Ian Bradford continue acting on behalf of MMC? I still felt that all this was somehow related to Carl and his murder. If Robert had been responsible for Carl's death, did it really matter now?

Yes. Yes, it did. If for no other reason than I needed to know.

Ten minutes later, I pulled up in front of Margie's Morsels and Marguerite came out and got into my Highlander. She passed a to-go cup to me.

"Noah said this is to make up for his last concoction. It's a white chocolate mocha."

"Thanks." I took a sip. "This is much better." I set it in the cupholder and pulled back onto the street. I had entered Robert's home address into the navigation system before I left for the hardware store and I pressed start on the screen.

While I drove, I told Marguerite that Daniel had finally told me about what happened ten years ago.

"I'm glad," Marguerite said. "I wanted to tell you, really I did."

"You should have. That whole not wanting to burden me was stupid."

"It wasn't just that. Daniel doesn't like talking about himself."

"I noticed."

Marguerite was silent for a moment. "How are the two of you getting along? Daniel's a really good guy."

Marguerite had put emphasis on the word *really*. There was only one reason she'd do that. "I hope you're not trying to fix us up."

"Me? Why would I do that?"

"Why indeed," I said. "Mar, you are not to play matchmaker here. I'm not ready. I loved Brian with all my heart. I know the general wisdom is to move on, but I can't. Not yet."

"I'm sorry," she said. "I won't mention it again."

I glanced over and gave her a smile. "I know you're only looking out for me."

She grinned. "And don't you forget it."

A few minutes later we reached the townhouse development where Robert and Cindy lived. I pulled into an empty spot, and Marguerite and I walked up the steps to their townhouse. I rang the bell but there was no answer. I repeated it two more times. Either she wasn't there, or she didn't want visitors.

"Now what?" Marguerite asked.

"I don't know. I wanted to offer my support. Maybe we should stop at the office and talk to Robert's partner. He might know how we can help."

"Good idea."

We got back on the road and I drove to the law office. The office complex didn't seem any busier than it had on my last visit. There was no one in the reception area when we entered the office, which was no surprise. Ian Bradford's office was right next to the reception area. His door was open, but he wasn't at his desk.

It was so quiet I felt compelled to whisper. "I guess no one's here. It's odd they'd leave the front door unlocked." Just then I heard a noise that sounded like it was coming from Robert's office at the end of the hall. I headed that way with Marguerite right behind me. When I reached the open doorway, I stopped suddenly.

Ian Bradford wasn't alone in the office. Cindy Larabee was in his arms and he was definitely offering her more than his condolences.

Chapter Sixteen

Marguerite and I backed up as quietly as we could. As soon as we were outside, Marguerite said, "Wow."

"I sure didn't expect that." We got back into my SUV.

"I wonder how long it's been going on," Marguerite said. "She didn't look much like a grieving widow."

"If it's been going on a while," I said. "I wonder if Robert knew about it. Maybe he really was leaving town."

"Would he leave his law practice because his wife was screwing around? Wouldn't he just boot her out and fire his partner?"

I pulled out of the parking lot. "This could be a heat of the moment sort of thing. Cindy was upset and crying, Ian consoled her, and what began as a comforting hug turned into a passionate kiss."

"I guess."

"I'm not going to judge her. For all we know she pushed him away and slapped him after we left."

"Or they had hot sex right there on her husband's desk," Marguerite said.

I couldn't help laughing. "You're terrible!"

Marguerite shrugged. "So are you or you wouldn't be laughing."

I dropped Marguerite off at her place and headed home. I didn't know what to make of the situation. I did know one thing, though—the next time I wanted to talk to Cindy I'd definitely call first.

*　*　*

I hadn't been home long when my phone rang. The area code wasn't local, and I almost didn't answer but was glad I did when the call turned out to be from Mike Thompson's father. "I'm glad you called," I said. "I'm sorry to bother you."

"No bother at all," Mr. Thompson said. "Mike told me you're Stan's niece. I was surprised you took over his orchard. I'd have thought he'd have sold it like I did my farm. Best decision I ever made."

"That's what I want to ask you about. I received an offer for my property and I've been trying to find some information about the potential buyer, with limited results. From what I've learned it's a company by the name of MMC, and I understand that's who bought your farm."

"Yep. That's the buyer. I never met anyone in person. Robert Larabee handled the closing and we did all the paperwork digitally. I did talk to someone on the phone from MMC at one point, but I don't remember his name. Nice fellow, though."

"Would you happen to still have that phone number?" I asked. That would be some progress anyway.

"I don't think I have it in my phone but it might be in some of the sales documents. I can take a look. It might take me a couple of days. I have to figure out what box they're in. We haven't unpacked everything yet."

"There's no rush, and I do appreciate it."

We chatted for a few minutes about my uncle and I thanked him again. A phone number wasn't much, but it would be more than I currently had.

After a dinner of boxed macaroni and cheese, Blossom and I sat on the couch. I turned on the TV and flipped through channels and stopped on a rerun of an old sitcom. I couldn't concentrate, though. My thoughts jumped from one thing to another. In my gut I knew Carl's money, his murder, the properties being bought, Robert, and the mysterious MMC were related somehow. But how? Maybe if I wrote it all down I'd figure it out.

I went upstairs and opened a carton that I'd packed with a few notebooks, pens, and pencils. I took one of the notebooks and a pen downstairs and sat down beside Blossom on the sofa. She meowed at me for disturbing her. I scratched her head, then opened the notebook. I'd start by listing what I knew in order.

The day after I arrived in Orchardville, I met with Carl and he showed me the barn. He'd used his own money for much of the restoration. At the time I worried about it, knowing he didn't make that much managing the orchard. I wrote a check to reimburse him. Next I saw him arguing with Jack Riggs. Carl told him he'd regret his decision. When I asked Jack if there was a problem, he said it wasn't anything he couldn't handle.

Then I found Carl in his cabin and was questioned by Scott. I had an alibi because I'd dined with Rudy and Ruth the previous night. When I began cleaning out Carl's cabin, Daniel and I found bank statements and a topographic map of the area. Someone had been paying Carl lots of money, either because he was blackmailing them or they were paying him to keep quiet about something.

This was the key. What was he being paid to keep quiet about? The topographic map showed the properties in the area, including this one. Had Carl learned about MMC and why they were buying up land?

Robert certainly had to be in on it all. He'd been the one present-ing the offers to the landowners and taking care of the closings. And now it would likely all come to a screeching halt because he was dead. Despite there being no evidence supporting Cherry Perry's story of seeing Carl and Robert arguing, I believed it. It made perfect sense and fit with what I knew so far. Either Carl wanted more money or he had threatened to tell what he knew. Or both.

I hadn't made any progress finding out anything about MMC other than Mr. Thompson possibly having a phone number for some-one there. I had a sudden thought. Maybe I'd been going about this all wrong. I thought about the map again. Why did Carl have that map in the freezer with his bank statements? It had to be important. What was so special about this land that someone had to have it? This area was mostly orchards and farms. It was obvious MMC wasn't buying the properties to continue farming. As of now, they hadn't done anything at all with the land. Maybe they were waiting to own all the properties first. I asked myself again what was so spe-cial about this land? I didn't have an answer. But I was determined to find one.

* * *

First thing in the morning I called Daniel.

"Are you all right?" He sounded worried.

"I'm fine," I said. "I might have figured some things out last night, and I'd like to run them past you."

"Have you had breakfast yet?"

"No, I haven't."

"I was just going to scramble some eggs. If you want to come over, I'll be happy to share."

"That's not necessary. I don't want you to go to any trouble."

"It's no trouble. Sometimes I like to cook, and you have to eat."

Daniel finally talked me into it, and ten minutes later I pulled up in front of his house. It wasn't anything like I'd expected. Most of the homes around here were traditional farmhouse types. Daniel's house was a log home stained a rich caramel. One side rose to a peak and featured a wall of windows. The other side was a single story and looked more cabin-like. The porch wrapped around to the back of the house and featured a log-topped black metal railing.

He opened the front door before I reached it. "Welcome."

"Your house is beautiful." I stepped into a two-story-tall great room. The living area held a brown leather sofa and two chairs. There was a stone fireplace with a woodstove insert on one wall. The kitchen was to the right and featured light hickory cabinets and a black countertop. To the back of the great room was a staircase leading to a loft.

"Thanks." He closed the door behind me. "The original house was just the one-story part and I added the rest."

"All by yourself?"

"Pretty much." He smiled. "I like to keep busy."

He led me to the kitchen and I took a seat at the island that doubled as his table. He poured two cups of coffee and slid ham and cheese omelets onto two plates.

"That's a little fancier than scrambled eggs," I said. "You went to too much trouble."

"There's milk in the fridge if you need it for your coffee."

I retrieved the milk and we both sat down.

"So what did you figure out?" he asked.

"First, I have to tell you what Marguerite and I did."

"Uh-oh. That doesn't sound good."

I laughed. "We didn't get in any trouble. But if we do, I know who to call to bail us out."

"I knew I shouldn't have told you I was a former cop."

In between bites, I told him about our visit to the law office and what we had witnessed.

"Interesting," he said.

I couldn't read his face. I then launched into what I'd come up with the previous night. "That map has to have some significance."

"I think you're right," he said. "We'll have to take a closer look at it." He got up and took our empty plates to the sink.

I grabbed my purse from the chair. "I brought it with me." I retrieved it and spread it out in front of us. Daniel pointed out the various properties like he had before. There wasn't anything we hadn't noticed earlier. Disappointed, I folded it up.

I told him about talking to Mr. Thompson.

"Well, that's something at least. If he comes up with a phone number that's a good place to start."

"I know there wasn't anything on the property website, but what if I visit the county offices tomorrow and see if there's something on the deeds?"

"That's a good idea."

Daniel poured us both another cup of coffee. "Let's take them over there." He pointed to the sofa and chairs.

I sat on the sofa and Daniel took a chair. The leather was buttery soft, and the cushioning was perfect. "Wow, this is really comfortable," I said. "I may have to rethink just getting slipcovers for Uncle Stan's furniture."

"There's an outlet store not far from here. You can get stuff for a reasonable price."

"I'll have to check it out." I sipped my coffee.

"I never met your grandmother," Daniel said. "What was she like?"

I smiled. "Grandma was great. She was a no-nonsense type of person. I don't think anyone could pull anything over on her. Believe me, I tried. I know my mother tried. That's why—" I stopped.

"Why what?"

"You don't really want to hear it."

"Of course I do. I wouldn't ask if I didn't."

"That's why Mom broke ties with Grandma." I told him what Ruth and Rudy had revealed. "I never knew what happened. Mom refused to talk about it. I missed out on so much because of it." I gave him a little smile. "But like Rudy said, I'm home now and that's all that matters."

"He's a wise man."

We finished our coffee, and before I left I told him I wanted to have a little memorial for Carl at the cidery on Wednesday. He said he'd be there.

That afternoon I went back into town. It was a beautiful day and Will Pearson was sitting on a chair in front of his store. He was dressed as General Grant and smoking a cigar. He stood and bowed as I approached. "Good afternoon," he said.

I returned his greeting.

"I heard about Robert Larabee," he said. "Damn shame."

"Yes, it is."

"What brings you to town today? I have some new things I can show you if you're interested."

I hadn't intended to shop, but I did have a few questions for him. "I'll be happy to look at them."

We went inside the store and he showed me some antique baskets he had picked up at a flea market the previous day. I ended up buying three. I'd hang them on one of the walls in the cidery and fill them with silk flowers or greens. Another customer came in and I browsed while Will waited on him. I spotted a few maps that I hadn't noticed before, hanging on a wall. Two were of the Gettysburg battlefield, but the third appeared to be a map of the Orchardville area. It was a bit faded and the glass in the frame was dusty, which made it hard to read.

When the other customer left, Will came over to me. "Do you like maps?" he asked.

I pointed to the one I'd been trying to read. "This one is interesting."

"Let me get it down for you." Will lifted it from the hanger on the wall and carried it over to the counter. "Sorry about the dust. That was one of the other things I picked up yesterday." He grabbed a paper towel and some glass cleaner and cleaned the glass. "That's better."

The map was indeed of the Orchardville area. The town itself was in the upper right of the map and although the date at the bottom was 1910, I recognized some of the names on the outlying properties—Thompson, Freeman, and even my grandfather's name, Owens. "I love this," I said.

"It is pretty cool," Will said.

I noticed some odd markings in three places. There were two lines with something that looked like a roof over them. I pointed to the one nearest the Thompson farm. "Do you know what these things are? They look almost like little houses."

"Hmm. Interesting. I didn't notice those before." He took a closer look. He slid his index finger across the glass to a spot on the far side of the Freeman place. "There's one over here too." He suddenly straightened up and snapped his fingers. "I bet they're marking the Reclamation."

"Reclamation? What's that?"

"The old Reclamation Mine."

Chapter Seventeen

"A mine? I've never heard of a mine around here," I said. "No one has ever even mentioned one."

"It closed in 1920, so a lot of folks don't remember it or don't know about it. Stan would have. He was the right generation."

I asked Will what he knew about it.

"Not much," he said. "My great-grandfather worked in it—or so the story goes. The Reclamation opened back in the late 1800s when Silas Gardner found gold and copper on his property when he was tilling his field or digging something or other. I don't remember exactly. I'm sure he thought he hit it big, but by the early part of the twentieth century any gold was depleted and it wasn't worth what it cost to mine any remaining copper, so the mine closed."

"Where was the Gardner property?" I asked.

Will studied the map. "I'm not sure exactly, but I think it was around here." He pointed to a spot northwest of the former Thompson farm.

I told him I wanted to buy the framed map and he quoted a price higher than I thought it was worth, but I purchased it anyway. I wanted to do some research on it, but it was possible this old abandoned mine had something to do with the sales of the local properties.

Before I left the store, I invited Will to Carl's wake, but he declined. I stopped in a few other stores on the way home and invited those who knew Carl to come. After that, I took my purchases home. I unwrapped the framed map and set it on the coffee table.

I wasn't particularly hungry, so I opened a can of chicken noodle soup for dinner. After I ate and washed the few dishes, I went to the living room and called the Millers to ask them to the wake. Ruth picked up on the third ring. I told her my plans.

"Rudy will be at the store," she said, "but I would love to come. I didn't know Carl as well as some—and I'm sure you've heard this a dozen times—he was good to Stan."

"I'm glad you'll be there," I said.

"It will give me a chance to see your new enterprise. What can I bring?"

"Just yourself. Marguerite has it covered. I don't expect a big turn-out so she's bringing some snacks."

As we chatted, my gaze kept straying to my new map. Ruth had lived in Orchardville all her life. She might know more about the Reclamation mine than Will had. I asked if she'd heard of it.

"Oh my. I haven't heard that name in a long time," she said. "I think Rudy's grandfather worked there for a bit before he opened the grocery store. Where did you hear about the mine?"

I told her about finding the map in Will's store.

"That was quite a find."

"It was," I said. I told her about the topographic map I'd found at Carl's without mentioning the bank statements. I decided not to say anything about the sales or the offer I'd received until I knew more about what was going on. "I'm really interested in the history of this area and the mine." It was true, I just wasn't telling the whole story. "What can you tell me about it?"

"Rudy knows more about it than I do," Ruth said. "Why don't you come to dinner again and you can ask him."

"I have a better idea. I've been meaning to have you two over, so why don't you come here for dinner tomorrow or Tuesday night?" We went back and forth about which one of us should be hosting. I finally said that Grandma would have been appalled I hadn't reciprocated.

"When you put it that way, I guess I'll have to accept. But I insist on bringing something. How about dessert?"

"That would be fine." We settled on tomorrow evening. Now I just had to figure out what to make.

*   *   *

Monday morning was rainy and chilly, so instead of my usual walk to the barn, I decided to drive. The rain and cold made me achy in all the places that had been put together through the miracle of modern medicine. It was a good day to stay inside. I had decided to make penne with meat sauce for dinner with Ruth and Rudy, so before I left the house I pulled out my old slow cooker and dumped in the ingredients for sauce. I could never understand buying sauce in a jar when it was so easy to make. I browned the ground beef, added chopped onions and peppers and mixed it all together in the slow cooker. After that I grabbed my laptop and headed out.

I still had plenty to do in the cidery even though the cider wouldn't be ready to rack to another tank for secondary fermentation for at least a few more days. It was too bad I wouldn't have anything ready for Carl's wake. I started a new batch in one of the empty tanks. I planned on staggering batches a week apart so I'd always have a variety to keg, and eventually bottle or can for takeout.

When I finished cleaning up, I sat down at a table and opened my laptop. I typed Reclamation Mine into the search engine and the first thing that came up was a Wikipedia article. I figured that was a good place to start. The history was similar to what Will Pearson had told me. It opened around 1880 on property owned by Silas Gardner and closed in 1920. The gold removed from the mine had been minimal, and at the time it had been too costly to mine any remaining copper. Silas Gardner's property had been sold at sheriff's sale the following year. He'd sunk everything he owned into the mine. I felt kind of bad for Silas. He probably had dreams of being rich and instead ended up penniless. I wondered what he'd done after that. I googled his name but only came up with a brief obituary from a Harrisburg paper in 1922. He'd left behind a wife, a son, and a daughter.

Other than Wikipedia, the only mention of the Reclamation Mine was one sentence in an obscure document on the geology of the area on the Pennsylvania Department of Conservation and Natural Resources website. It basically just stated that it had existed for a brief time. I was just about to return to Google when Daniel came in.

"Need any help today?" He sat down across from me. "Still researching properties?"

"I am," I said. "Wait till you hear what I found." I told him about the map I'd bought at Blue and Gray Collectibles and the Reclamation Mine. "I'm trying to find more information on it. It looks like it might have run under some of the properties that MMC is snatching up."

"I never heard anything about a mine nearby. It kind of makes sense, though. There was one close to Gettysburg—I think in Hunterstown. We're not all that far away."

I pulled up the Wikipedia article so he could read it. "I'm wondering if someone thinks there's still gold or copper down there and is planning on mining it again."

"Then why not just buy the mineral rights?" Daniel said.

"Probably because no one wants someone digging under their property. I know I wouldn't want to have to worry about subsidence."

"True. Neither would I." He finished reading the article. "Have you contacted anyone at the DCNR?"

I shook my head. "All I found on their site was an article on the geology of the area with a brief mention of the mine."

"I'd like to take a look at the map when you get a chance."

"It's back at the house, but I can show it to you now if you have time." It was almost lunchtime anyway so he followed me home. As soon as we walked inside, the aroma of the sauce that had been simmering all morning made my mouth water.

"Something smells delicious," Daniel said. "Spaghetti sauce?"

"Yes. Ruth and Rudy are coming for dinner tonight."

"I'm envious. I love pasta in any shape or form."

"Why don't you join us, then? There will be plenty. And Ruth is bringing dessert."

"Are you sure?" he said. "I don't want to interfere."

"You're not interfering. Besides, Rudy might know something about the mine. Ruth said his grandfather worked there before he went into the grocery business."

"I'll bring bread and a bottle of wine."

With that settled I showed him the framed map that was still on the coffee table. I offered to make sandwiches while he looked at the map. Five minutes later I carried our plates to the living room.

"Thanks," Daniel said. He pointed to the place on the map marked Gardner. "You said the Gardner property was sold at sheriff's sale? That's right in the middle of where Morrison Agricultural Products is located now."

I sat beside him on the couch. "How long has the company been there? I wonder if that's who bought it back then."

"That would be easy enough to find out," Daniel said. He took out his phone and pulled up the Morrison website. "Here we go. The company was founded in 1918 in Albert Morrison Senior's barn."

"So where was his barn?" I asked. "His name isn't on the map."

"It doesn't say." He scrolled down. "By 1920, the company needed to expand and they purchased the land where their manufacturing facility sits today."

"The former Gardner farm," I said.

"Looks like it."

"So Gardner opens a mine when he finds gold or copper on his property. It isn't all that profitable and goes belly up in 1920. Then Morrison buys the property at sheriff's sale and expands his agricultural business."

"That about sums it up," Daniel said.

I continued. "And now someone wants to buy land near where the mine used to be. Robert was acting on behalf of something called MMC and making offers for more than the properties were worth. Somehow Carl must have found out whatever was going on and got paid to keep quiet."

"And if Carl's conscience got the better of him, he was murdered before he could talk," Daniel said.

"Could it have been Robert?"

"It's possible," Daniel said. "It fits. Scott is going over his finances, so he'll know soon enough. It might not matter now that Robert is dead."

"I doubt that MMC is going to give up just because their go-between is dead."

"True."

Something struck me suddenly. I put my unfinished sandwich down on my plate. "Morrison."

"What about it?" Daniel asked.

"What if one of the Ms in MMC stands for Morrison?"

"Go on."

"Morrison owns some of the land where the mine was. What if someone at the company found out there's still gold down there? They want all the land instead of just the mineral rights because they don't want anyone to know about it."

"But the mine closed because the gold had been depleted," Daniel said.

I shrugged, undeterred. "That was over a hundred years ago. There are probably better ways to determine what's actually there and new ways to get it out."

Daniel leaned forward and looked at the map again. He pointed to the little marks that showed where entrances to the mine may once have been, then to the area marked *Owens*—my grandparent's name. He looked at me.

He didn't have to say a word. My property was right in the middle of those markings.

Chapter Eighteen

"No wonder Robert thought I should sell this place," I said. "If MMC is planning to open the mine again, they wouldn't want me right in the middle of it. I can't believe they'd be allowed to get away with it. There has to be some kind of environmental law against this sort of thing."

"There also have to be permits—state, county, and maybe local," Daniel said.

"With all the secrecy, though, maybe they're trying to do it without bothering with permits. As soon as they get a permit, the clerk tells a buddy, who tells another buddy, and before you know it, it's all over the news."

"Maybe. I know someone who works for the Pennsylvania Department of Environmental Protection. I'll see what I can find out." He pushed off the couch. "I'm going to run this past Scott, too, and see what he can tell me about Morrison Agricultural."

I got to my feet. "Thanks." I walked him to the door, then put our lunch dishes in the sink. I tossed my half-eaten sandwich in the garbage. I wasn't hungry anymore. If our theories were correct, someone was out to destroy everything my grandparents had built on this land—acres of fruit trees, this house, my cidery. All for what? A little gold, or maybe copper?

I thought about Carl and wondered what exactly he had known about all this. Had Robert tried to get Uncle Stan to sell before he died, knowing that I'd inherit? After all, what city girl would want an orchard and an old farmhouse?

Robert hadn't counted on *this* city girl. Digging a mine under my family property? I wasn't going to let that happen.

* * *

I spent the rest of the afternoon preparing for that evening's dinner. Ruth and Rudy's house was clean enough to eat off the floors, so I felt obligated to at least dust and sweep. When everything was tolerably clean, I went to the large grocery store five miles away and bought a box of penne pasta, bagged salad, some dressing, and a few other things I was out of. I was glad I had time for a quick nap when I got home.

I tried to put everything that had happened since I arrived in Orchardville out of my mind, but I couldn't. It was all so confusing. Every time I felt like I was on the verge of figuring it all out, there was some little tidbit just out of reach, which made me doubt everything I'd been thinking. Maybe Carl's killer wasn't anyone connected to the property sales. Maybe it was some random person who broke in looking for who knows what. Besides, what made me think I could solve something the police couldn't? Both Scott and Daniel had experience in solving crimes. I didn't. I kept asking myself why I was compelled to look into this in the first place. I should leave it to the police, especially now that Robert was dead. If he was the one who killed Carl, there was no point in pursuing it.

But what if it wasn't Robert? With everything I'd learned in the last couple of days, there was a good chance it was someone at MMC. I had no idea how to learn who that might be.

I didn't get a chance to ponder it any further. There was a knock at the door just as I put the pasta into the pot of boiling water. I gave it a quick stir, turned the heat down a little so it didn't boil over, and answered the door.

Ruth and Rudy were right on time. Ruth was carrying a large plate that held cupcakes and cookies. She passed it to me.

"Thank you for inviting us," she said.

Rudy chimed in. "I've been looking forward to this all day."

While I hung their jackets on the coat rack beside the front door, they stood in the foyer and looked around. Ruth had tears in her eyes.

"It's just like I remembered," she said. "I can picture your grand-mother walking down those stairs like it was yesterday. Melinda would be so happy you're here."

"She certainly would," Rudy said. He sniffed the air. "Something smells good."

"I hope it'll be good. Make yourselves at home while I take these to the kitchen and check on the pasta."

"I'll help," Ruth said, following me to the kitchen. "Oh my. Noth-ing has changed at all in here! The old cabinets, and Melinda's table and chairs. I don't know what I expected. I should have known Stan wouldn't have remodeled it. I guess building the house was enough for him. After that, he spent all his time out in the orchard."

I set the dessert plate on the counter. "I don't plan on changing it—at least for now. It brings back a lot of memories." I opened the refrigerator and got out the salad that I'd already dumped from the bag into the bowl. It was silly, but I hadn't wanted Ruth to know the salad had come from a bag.

"Let me take that," Ruth said.

I passed it to her and retrieved the salad dressing from the fridge. We took it to the dining room. "I'm even using Grandma's good dishes."

Ruth put the salad on the table. "Four places?"

"Daniel Martinez is joining us." I was momentarily saved from any questions by the knock on the door. I headed that way, but Rudy beat me to it.

"Daniel," Rudy said. "This is a surprise. I didn't know you were coming."

"I sort of invited myself after I got a whiff of that spaghetti sauce earlier."

Ruth kept glancing back and forth between Daniel and me. I think she was trying to guess if there was anything going on there. I'd have to put a stop to any attempted matchmaking like I had done with Marguerite.

"Daniel's been helping me at the cidery and the orchard," I said. "He found me a manager—two of them, actually." I told them about hiring the Diaz brothers for the orchard and cidery.

It wasn't long before we were all seated at the table. We chatted throughout dinner, and afterward I made coffee and we had dessert in the living room. Once we were settled, I asked Rudy about the Reclamation Mine.

"Ruth mentioned you found an old map or something," he said.

"Yes." I got up and pulled out the map that I'd shoved behind the couch. I leaned it against the coffee table. "It's dated 1910 and shows some of the properties around here. Will Pearson said those marks that look like little houses might be the mine entrances."

Rudy studied it. "I do believe that's correct. I guess Ruth told you my grandfather worked there, probably around the same time as that map was drawn. He opened his grocery store in 1919. The Reclamation wasn't doing well the last few years it was open and the owner had to let some of the employees go. Pop—that's what we called my grandfather—figured the grocery business was more stable because people always needed food. My dad expanded it and passed it on to me."

"Kate didn't ask you about the store, dear," Ruth said.

I laughed. "That's all right. I don't mind."

Rudy smiled. "I guess I got a little sidetracked. What do you want to know?"

"I'm wondering how large the mine was—how far it extended."

"I don't know for sure," he said. "There were three entrances where it's marked on the map but I don't think it was dug very far. I doubt it came this far if you're worried about subsidence."

"I'm not worried," I said.

Rudy continued. "From what I remember my grandfather saying, very little gold was found after the first few years. They managed to get some copper out, but they would have either had to dig much deeper or do open pit mining like they do with coal in parts of the state."

I remembered an area outside of Pittsburgh where open pit mining had been done. A large hill eventually turned into an ugly valley. It was an eyesore and then some. Something like that would be devastating to the farms and orchards here. I looked across the room at Daniel. He seemed to be thinking the same thing.

"Why didn't they do open pit at the Reclamation?" Daniel asked.

"Silas Gardner had been a farmer at heart despite his mining interest. He didn't want to destroy the land. He closed the mine and went bankrupt. He took his own life not long after he lost his land to foreclosure."

"That's so sad," I said.

"It is," Ruth said. "He lost everything."

Rudy was more matter-of-fact about it. "He shouldn't have been so greedy. If he'd been content with what he had, that land might still be a farm."

"What do you know about Morrison Agricultural—the company that bought his property?" Daniel asked.

"Not a lot," Rudy said. "I never gave it much thought. It's one of those places that's always been there. Even though I'd prefer farmland there, the company employs a lot of folks. I know they make natural fertilizer and such—supposedly it's environmentally friendly, whatever that means."

"Do you know who owns the company?" I asked.

"I believe it's Albert Morrison," he said.

"Wasn't that the name of the guy who started the company?" I said. "It must be one of his descendants."

Rudy nodded. "He comes into the store on occasion. I think he's actually Morrison the fourth. Or maybe the third. I can't remember which."

"Why are you so interested?" Ruth asked.

I didn't want to tell her the whole story, so I opted for a half-truth. "I'm trying to learn all about this area and its history. I missed out on a lot after I wasn't allowed to visit anymore. I'm grateful that Uncle Stan remembered me and I want to do right by him and Grandma."

Ruth reached over and patted my hand. "They would both be so proud of you."

I nodded, because words seemed to have suddenly gotten stuck in my throat. We chatted for a while about Grandma and Uncle Stan. Ruth offered to help clean up before they left, but I told her it wasn't necessary. As I opened the door to walk outside with Ruth and Rudy, Daniel's phone rang.

He checked the screen. "I have to get this."

I continued outside with my guests while Daniel stayed in the foyer and answered his phone. The Millers got into their car and I waved goodbye, then went back inside.

Daniel thanked whoever was on the other end of the line and pocketed his phone. "That was my former colleague in Harrisburg. They found paint transfer on Larabee's car."

I was puzzled. "Paint transfer?"

He nodded. "Larabee's accident wasn't an accident. There's evidence his vehicle was forced off the road. He was murdered."

Chapter Nineteen

"Oh my God." I sank into a chair. "What in the world is going on?"

"I wish I knew," Daniel said.

"They don't think he was accidentally forced off the road? Like someone hit him and just left?"

"Not according to what I was just told."

"I don't understand any of this," I said. "If Robert was facilitating the property sales, why kill him? It doesn't make sense."

"I know." His phone rang again. "It's Scott."

While Daniel talked to Scott, I tried to come up with a reason why Robert had been killed. The only thing I could think of was that Robert had wanted out. Out of what, though? Maybe he hadn't known why MMC wanted the properties. Maybe he found out they wanted to begin mining again and the land would be destroyed. That didn't make sense, though. I hadn't known Robert that well, but he didn't appear to care one way or another about land use. He had been a good attorney and I can't imagine him not being informed before he took on a client.

"Scott and I are going to Harrisburg tomorrow to fill the investigators in on what's been going on here," Daniel said as he stuffed his phone back into his pocket. "Are you all right? Scott can go alone if you need me to stick around."

"I'm okay. Just confused at the moment."

"Do you need help cleaning up?" he asked.

I shook my head. "No. I may leave the dishes until morning. You should take some of Ruth's cookies."

"I think I will."

We went to the kitchen and I dropped a dozen or more cookies into a plastic bag, then I walked him to the door.

"Thanks for dinner," he said.

"You're welcome."

Daniel looked at me for a moment. He opened his mouth and closed it like he was going to say something then changed his mind. Instead, he reached up and squeezed my shoulder. "Good night."

I watched him get into his truck, then closed and locked the door. My shoulder where he'd squeezed it felt warm. I'd seen that look before, but it had been ages ago. Brian had looked at me like that on our third date. "I'm not ready," I whispered to myself. "It's too soon."

Babe, you gotta let go. I could still hear Brian's voice in my head.

"I'm not ready," I whispered again. Brian would have told me that was a load of bull. That he was gone and wasn't coming back. That he wanted me to live my life and be happy. "I am happy," I said aloud. Most of the time, anyway. I turned out the lights and headed upstairs.

I tried not to think about anything once I was in bed. As I dozed off a thought hit me and I was wide awake again. What if Robert's murder wasn't related to the properties at all? His wife was having an affair with his business partner—at least that's what it had looked like when Marguerite and I saw them together. She would certainly benefit from his death. I needed to pay a visit to Cindy Larabee.

* * *

At ten the next morning, I pulled into the parking lot of the Larabee law office. I parked across from the few other cars so I could walk past and check for damage. I didn't know what kind of vehicle Cindy drove, but there would be extensive damage if she'd forced an Escalade off the road. None of the cars had any damage. So much for that theory.

Cindy was at her desk when I entered. There was a box of tissues beside her and it looked like she'd been crying. She pushed the box aside when she saw me and rose to her feet.

"I thought I'd stop and offer my condolences," I said.

She came around the desk and took one of my hands in hers and squeezed it. "Thank you so much. I know I shouldn't be here, but I can't stand being at home. I need to keep busy."

"I understand. Is there anything I can do?"

"There's nothing to be done at the moment, but thank you for asking. Ian's helping me with arrangements now that . . . now that the police have released Robert's body. Ian has been wonderful. I don't know what I would have done without him."

I was glad I hadn't asked Marguerite to come with me. She would have said something to me under her breath about that. "Have the police told you what happened?"

Cindy nodded. "I don't quite understand it all. At first they said he went over an embankment and now they're saying someone hit him to make the car go over. Who would do something like that? Who would cause an accident and leave a man to die?" She sobbed and reached for a tissue.

Cindy certainly seemed distraught, but I couldn't tell if it was real or an act. I thought back to the kiss that Marguerite and I had witnessed. If she was having an affair with her husband's law partner, it was possible this was all a performance. She very well could have killed, or had her husband killed. Even so, there was still a good chance

Robert's death was related to MMC and the properties being bought. If MMC was somehow connected to Morrison Agricultural, I knew who I needed to talk to next.

* * *

After stopping at the barn and checking the tanks, I headed into town. It was lunchtime so I went to Margie's Morsels. There was a tour bus in the parking lot, which didn't bode well for Marguerite having time to talk to me. The café was packed. I crossed the room and took the lone seat at the counter. "Hi, Noah. It's a little busy today," I said.

"Yeah. I'm not real busy, though. Most of these folks just ordered water or iced tea. The few coffee drinkers aren't into lattes. Marguerite, on the other hand, is running her butt off."

"Does she need help?" I asked.

"Nah. She loves it. Kris and Mary are here, too. They can handle it. What can I get you?"

Since Noah didn't seem happy having to serve plain, old coffee, I opted for an iced caramel macchiato.

He grinned. "Feeling sorry for me, I see."

"Maybe."

Marguerite came out of the kitchen with a tray of full plates. "Hey, Kate. Be with you in minute." She expertly served a table of six, then came around the counter. "I hear you cooked yesterday and everyone lived to tell about it."

"Ha, very funny," I said. "I'm a good cook. I just don't do it that often. Who squealed?"

"Rudy stopped in on his way to the store this morning. He said Daniel was there."

Marguerite tried to sound casual, but there was a definite tone that told me she was fishing. I wouldn't give in to her curiosity.

"Yeah. He mentioned he loved spaghetti and practically invited himself. I figured it wouldn't hurt to feed him, especially after he made us breakfast at his house the other day."

"Wait. Stop the presses. You were at his place for breakfast?"

I wanted to kick myself. I shouldn't have said that. Now she would definitely get the wrong idea.

"You spent the night there?" she asked.

"No! Absolutely not!" If I shook my head any harder I'd strain my neck. "I called him with a question and he happened to be making breakfast, so he invited me over. That's it."

"Uh-huh." Marguerite had a big grin on her face.

I felt my face flushing. "It's true. Ask Daniel."

"Oh, I will. Believe me."

I changed the subject. "How does a starving cidery owner get some lunch around here?"

Ten minutes later she placed a cheeseburger and fries on the counter in front of me. We didn't get a chance to talk again because of the crowd. Before I left I flagged her down and told her to stop by later if she wasn't busy. If not, I'd see her tomorrow since she was bringing food for Carl's wake.

As I drove through town, I saw Renee coming out of ScentSations and honked. She waved me over. I found a spot to park and seconds later I met her on the sidewalk. "I heard about Robert Larabee," she said. "It's horrible."

"It is. I went to see his wife this morning. She seems really broken up." I didn't mention I wasn't sure that she really was.

"I can imagine. I wanted to tell you my father received another offer for his farm through the mail. It's even higher than the first offer, but I imagine with Robert Larabee's death, it doesn't matter anyway."

"I guess not," I said. "Robert has a law partner, so he might take over."

"Well, Dad won't sell no matter what." She smiled. "Eli tells me I inherited that bullheadedness from him."

"There are worse things to inherit."

"I also wanted to tell you I'll be going to Carl's wake tomorrow. Eli will cover the store for me. I have the centerpieces for your tables done, so I can bring them with me."

"That would be great." I spotted Cherry Perry heading our way. "Uh-oh."

Renee turned to look. "Crap."

Cherry pointed at me. "You! I need to talk to you."

Renee squeezed my elbow. "Lots of luck. I have to run." She turned and walked quickly in the opposite direction.

"Hi, Cherry," I said cordially.

"I told you there was a serial killer on the loose. Carl Randolph is dead. Now that lawyer fellow is dead too. I told the police, but they don't believe me. I told the chief he needs to call in the FBI."

"It's not a serial killer. Robert Larabee was in a car accident." I wasn't about to tell her someone forced him off the road. I could only imagine what she'd do with that information.

"That doesn't mean anything. You need to get the chief to call in the FBI before we're all killed."

I didn't know what to say to her. I was pretty sure I wouldn't convince her that her worries were unfounded. "I'll mention it to him."

She looked relieved. "Why don't you stop in the store and I'll give you some tea. It's on the house."

"Can I take a rain check?"

"It won't take long," she said.

Cherry sounded so hopeful I gave in. I wondered how much repeat business she had. She probably bent the ears of any customers she did have, and if she was on a rant about serial killers, they weren't likely to return.

The interior of CertainTea wasn't anything like I'd imagined. Vintage-looking shelves lined a wall that held baskets labeled with little blackboard-type tags. The baskets were filled with prepackaged teas of dozens of varieties. Lace tablecloths covered round tables throughout the store, showcasing beautiful teapots and cups. Another wall held tea accessories and jars filled with loose teas to make special blends. Soft music played over the sound system. It was peaceful, unlike its owner. I ended up choosing some peppermint tea and a chamomile blend. Cherry wasn't anywhere near as chatty and rambling in the store. She was knowledgeable about her products, and very professional. Maybe I was wrong about the repeat customers. She didn't mention serial killers once.

*　　*　　*

Back at the cidery, I set out some more tables for Carl's wake. There really wasn't a whole lot to do. There wouldn't be any type of religious service. I'd just say a few words and ask anyone who wanted to do the same. We'd have a few snacks, then everyone would go on their way. It wasn't much, but I didn't think Carl would have wanted a big send-off.

When I finished I looked up the phone number for Morrison Agricultural Products. There were no individual listings so I called the main number. I told the person who answered I'd like to speak to Albert Morrison. She transferred the call and the woman who picked up stated that Mr. Morrison wasn't in that day. I left my name and number and asked her to have him call me when he was back in the office.

With nothing left to do for a change, I headed home. Marguerite called to tell me she'd see me tomorrow—she was too tired to stop by tonight. I ate leftover pasta for dinner and spent a quiet evening doing some online shopping for slipcovers for the living room furniture. Once things were more settled, I'd check out the furniture outlet that Daniel had recommended. Slipcovers would do for now. Blossom and I were both asleep by ten.

The next morning I headed to the cidery a little earlier than usual. I checked the gauges on the fermentation tanks and everything was as it should be. I'd brought the framed map of the area with me and found a spot on one of the walls to hang it. It would make a nice conversation piece if nothing else. I was across the room looking to see that it was level when Renee arrived carrying a carton holding the centerpieces. She set the box down on a table.

"Is that a map of this area?" she asked.

"Yep."

Renee crossed the room to get a closer look. "This is really neat. It even shows the old mine entrance by our place."

Chapter Twenty

"You know about the mine?" I said.

"Sure. As kids we were always warned not to go near it. The entrance was boarded up and covered with vines and such, but of course we ignored the warnings. My friends and I had visions of finding something like Indiana Jones did. One of my friends even had a hat like Harrison Ford wore in the movie. I actually think he's an archaeologist now."

I laughed. "A real-life Indy. So what's it like? The mine, I mean."

"Dark, damp, and musty. You should talk to my dad about it. His grandfather worked there."

It seemed like a lot of that generation had done the same. "I'll do that."

"And talk to Will Pearson. He's done a lot of research on the mine. I think he was going to write a book about it."

I hid my surprise. "I'll do that." That was interesting. Will had never mentioned a book and he had played down how much he knew when I bought the map. That whole lightbulb-over-the-head moment had been an act. Why would he do that?

I didn't have time to think about it anymore because Marguerite arrived. Renee and I helped her set out the cheese and fruit trays she'd made. We didn't have a chance to talk because people began to arrive. It was a better turnout than I'd thought. Overall about a dozen people showed up, including Marguerite, Renee, Daniel, and Ruth. Even Jack Riggs came and said that he and Carl hadn't always been on the best of terms, but he knew Carl had been a good guy. It was nice to hear that.

Daniel and Marguerite stayed afterward to help put things back in order—not that there was that much to do. When we finished, Marguerite poured the coffee that remained in the urn she'd brought into three paper cups and we sat down at a table.

"That was nice," Marguerite said.

Daniel nodded. "Carl didn't like a fuss, but he would have been okay with this."

"He might have liked it better if I'd held it in the middle of the orchard," I said.

"Maybe not," Daniel said. "He wouldn't have liked people wandering all over the orchard."

I was dying to ask Daniel about his trip to Harrisburg the day before, but I wasn't sure how much he'd want to divulge to Marguerite. Instead, I told them about my visit to see Cindy Larabee and how distraught she'd seemed. "I'm not sure I believe it, though," I said. "I mean, it seemed genuine, but I just don't know."

"Maybe she's a good actress," Marguerite said.

"It's possible. I'd like to think the tears were real."

"Did she say anything about the clinch we saw her in?" Marguerite asked.

I shook my head. "I didn't mention it. All she said was that Ian was very helpful."

"I'll bet," Marguerite said.

Daniel pointed to the wall. "That's a great place for the map."

"What map?" Marguerite turned around to look. "The one you found at Carl's?"

"It's a different one." I filled her in. "I had just hung it up when Renee came in this morning. She said one of the entrances is near her dad's place and she and her friends used to play there when they were kids even though they were warned not to."

Marguerite nudged me. "Too bad we didn't know about it. We would have joined them."

"That's probably why Grandma never mentioned it. She knew we'd take it as a challenge." I went on with my story. "Renee said her great-grandfather worked at the mine and that I should talk to her dad about it. By the way, she also said he received another offer for his place in the mail for higher than the previous one."

"I'd like to see those papers if he still has them," Daniel said.

"I'll find out and we can go see him together tomorrow." I didn't so much as glance at Marguerite when I said it. I didn't want to see the expression on her face.

"I can't tomorrow," Daniel said. "I have a meeting with a potential new fruit buyer."

"If Mr. Freeman will part with the papers, I'll bring them home with me."

"I'd appreciate that."

"Did Renee say anything else?" Marguerite asked.

I nodded. "She told me I should talk to Will Pearson. She said he's done a lot of research on the mine and was planning to write a book on it. The funny thing is, he never mentioned that to me. He even played down what he knew."

"That's a little suspicious," Marguerite said. "Most people would jump at the chance to show their expertise. Especially Will. He's always correcting people on their so-called Civil War knowledge."

"And yet he sold the map to you," Daniel said.

"I guess he didn't need it for his research."

Marguerite's phone buzzed with a text message and she looked at the screen. "Gotta go. Duty calls. Apparently, we ran out of green peppers. I'll have to stop at the store on the way back."

After she left I asked, "Do you think Will is hiding something?"

"Maybe," Daniel said. His tone sounded like it was more than a possibility. "I'll have a chat with him."

"You miss it, don't you?" I said.

"Miss what?"

"Police work."

"Sometimes. But I have more than enough to keep me busy. It's all in the past, anyway."

"You could still get a desk job with the police, couldn't you?" I asked.

Daniel laughed. "Like I said before, I'd last about five minutes. I'm not cut out to sit still. I'm perfectly happy doing what I'm doing now."

I nodded. "Speaking of police work, what did you and Scott find out yesterday?"

"Not a whole lot. Mostly, Scott filled them in on his investigation. The only thing we got out of it was the info that the paint transfer came from a white vehicle—probably something large considering where the damage occurred. And it had to be big enough to push Larabee's Escalade off the road."

"So the question is, who drives a large, white vehicle?"

"And who had a motive to kill Larabee?" Daniel added.

Big questions with no answers. At least not yet.

* * *

My phone rang on my walk home. I was surprised to see Larabee Law on the caller ID. I pressed the button to answer the call.

"Hi, Kate," Cindy Larabee said. "I'm sorry to bother you."

"It's no bother. How are you?"

"A little better than when we spoke. It's going to be an adjustment."

"It's definitely an adjustment."

"I'm glad I have this job to keep me occupied. I'd go crazy sitting at home thinking about Robert. All I want to do is cry, and I can't keep doing that."

Maybe my doubts about her grief were unfounded.

"Anyway, I thought I'd better give you a call about something." she said. "It has to do with your great-uncle's estate."

"Really? I thought everything was finalized with the estate."

"Apparently not everything," Cindy said. "I was gathering up some things from Robert's files to pass on to Ian and I found a document that you need to see. It's important."

"Another document? What is it?" I asked.

"I'd rather you see it for yourself."

"I'm free the rest of the day," I said.

"I can't this afternoon. Would tomorrow be all right?"

We made the appointment for two o'clock the following day. I couldn't imagine what she had found. Robert had given me copies of everything. There was nothing missing as far as I knew. When I got home I pulled out the accordion folder that held all the documents. I went through them one by one. I didn't see any problems. I put the folder away. I'd find out soon enough. It was certainly puzzling, though.

The next morning after checking on things at the cidery, I drove to the Freeman farm to see Renee's dad. He was sitting on the front porch when I pulled up.

"You're Renee's friend, the brewery lady," he said when I got out of the car.

I didn't correct him.

He pointed to the rocker next to him. "Take a load off."

"Thanks. It's a beautiful morning, isn't it?"

He grinned. "It's always a beautiful morning when I wake up. At my age, you never know."

"I guess none of us ever do," I said. "Renee told me you got another offer on this place."

"I did. Whoever's making these offers is an idiot. This place ain't worth what they're willing to pay. In cash, no less. Renee thinks I should take the money. I just can't do it."

"Some things are worth more than money."

"You're a smart gal," he said.

"I think I mentioned before that my attorney told me someone wanted to buy my orchard."

Mr. Freeman nodded. "I remember. We have the same lawyer. Or we did. I guess I'll have to deal with the partner now."

"Renee said the latest bid came through the mail," I said. "Did it come from the Larabee firm?"

"Nosiree. It came from some company. I still have the papers if you want to take a look."

"If you don't mind. I don't want you to go to any trouble."

Mr. Freeman was on his feet before I finished the sentence. "No trouble at all. Come on in."

I followed him inside where he pointed to a stack of mail on his kitchen table. He picked up a sheet of folded paper from the top of the pile and passed it to me. The letterhead read MMC, LLC, with an Orchardville post office box for an address. I wondered if it was possible to trace the owner of a box. The town was small and I'd bet whoever worked at the post office knew everyone who had a box. If I asked, the worst they could do was tell me they can't divulge the information. "Do you know anything about this company, MMC?" I asked.

"Not a thing. Orchardville ain't that big, and I never heard of it. If I wanted to sell, I'd need to know a heck of a lot more about it."

"Me too." I scrolled through the letter and stopped when I saw how much they wanted to pay. "Holy moly," I said. "That's a lot." No wonder Renee thought he should sell. "Are you sure you don't want to take them up on it?"

"I'm sure." He grinned. "I'm gonna put them off just to see how high they go. I'm ornery like that."

I laughed. "Keep me posted." I folded the letter. "Do you mind if I take this with me? I'd like to show it to someone."

"Go right ahead. It's gonna end up in the trash anyway."

"Thanks." I told him about the map I bought and that Renee had told me his grandfather worked in the mine.

"Yep. He worked there in the wintertime and worked the farm the rest of the year. I guess he did it for the extra money."

"What do you know about the mine?" I asked.

"I only know what my grandpa told me. He didn't like it much and he was glad when it closed. I don't know if Renee told you or not, but the old entrance is on the far side of that field over there." He pointed out the window.

I didn't mention that Renee had said she used to play there, but I'd bet he already knew about it. I didn't think anyone could get much past him. He was awfully sharp for someone ninety years old. We chatted for a few minutes, then I thanked him and left.

On the way back, I took a chance and stopped at the post office. It was in the same building as the police department and town office. Scott's door was closed and I could see him at his desk through the window. I didn't want to bother him, so I turned and walked into the post office. The sole employee was named Gretchen. I explained I was trying to find a person behind MMC. Unfortunately, she wouldn't budge and refused to divulge who paid the bill for Box 27.

I spent the remainder of the morning at the cidery. I sat with my laptop and planned out my cider batches for the rest of the year. I made a call to order more apple juice for next week when the first batch would finish and I could start another one. While I ate my lunch I set up the point of sale system and installed the cash drawer. It looked like everything was ready except the cider. *Soon*, I told myself. *Soon*.

* * *

I pulled into the parking lot of Larabee Law at five minutes to two. Cindy was at her desk and seemed much better than she had the other day.

"Robert's funeral will be tomorrow at ten if you can make it," she said. "I decided not to have a viewing or anything, but there will be a short service at Treetop Cemetery."

"I'll be there," I said.

"Ian thinks we should take a few days off after that."

I noticed she used *we* instead of *I*. Maybe there really was something going on between them. "It's a good idea. I'm sure it's been a stressful time. You need to take care of yourself."

She nodded. "Let's go back to Robert's office and I'll show you what I found."

I followed her down the hallway. Robert's office hadn't changed since my previous visit other than several stacks of folders on the top of the desk. Cindy took a seat in her late husband's chair and I sat in the same one I'd occupied before. She lifted a folder from the top of one of the stacks and opened it. "I don't know how it happened, but Robert missed something regarding the estate," she said.

"Like what? I went through all the paperwork yesterday after you called and there was nothing missing as far as I could tell. Everything had been executed."

Cindy lifted a document from the file and slid it across the desk to me. "Robert missed this one. I feel terrible about this, but it looks like you don't actually own your uncle's property."

Chapter
Twenty-One

"What do you mean I don't own the property?" I said. "Of course I do. I have all the paperwork."

"Except for this document," Cindy said. "Somehow this paper got misplaced, but it appears your uncle sold the property ."

"I don't believe that. Robert would have told me. I have the deed transfer papers and everything that goes with them. Besides, Uncle Stan clearly left everything to me in his will. There's nothing to indicate he sold it."

"I'm really sorry," Cindy said. "But according to this, your uncle sold it to one of Robert's clients two weeks before he died. That means the papers that you signed are null and void."

My stomach was in knots. How was this possible? Robert had been so meticulous with everything. He wouldn't have missed this. "I still don't believe it. I saw Robert just before he went out of town and he told me he had another offer for my place. Why would he do that if it had already been sold?"

"I don't know," Cindy said. "Other than Robert was very busy. He had a lot on his mind and hadn't been himself lately. It's possible he just forgot. All I know is what's on this paper. It's signed by both Robert and your uncle."

I picked up the document and flipped to the last page. There at the bottom were the two signatures. "It's not possible." I shook my head. "It's just not possible."

"I'm so sorry, Kate," Cindy said. "I know you had your heart set on opening your cider house. I guess you'll have to do that somewhere else. Once this is filed, you'll have more than enough for that. Maybe it's for the best. Robert always said the orchard was losing money."

"Robert was wrong. The orchard is not losing money."

Cindy ignored my comment. "There are three copies of this in the folder. It looks like one is for the buyer, one for the seller, and one for the recorder of deeds."

"I want all three copies," I said.

"I don't think that's allowed. I'll have to check with Ian when he gets back in town."

"You mean to tell me he doesn't know about this?"

Cindy's cheeks reddened. "I only found it yesterday. Ian hasn't been in the office. He'll be back in time for the funeral tomorrow. You can have your uncle's copy, but I should keep the others."

My shock over the situation finally turned to anger. "Right now, I am the owner of record and I'm not going to let anyone take my legacy away from me."

"I know this is hard for you, Kate. I'm really sorry."

"Hard doesn't begin to describe it," I said. I swallowed the words I wanted to say. Arguing more wouldn't do me any good. I picked up my copy of the papers and stormed out of the office. I got into my vehicle and slammed the door so hard the window rattled. Then I burst into tears. This couldn't be happening. Despite how it seemed, there was no way that document was legitimate. I had to prove it somehow.

By the time I got home I had calmed down somewhat. I got all my documents out again and spread them out on the dining room table.

The sales agreement Cindy had given me looked like a standard one. I was interrupted by a knock on the door. I went to answer it, hoping whoever it was didn't notice my bloodshot eyes and red nose.

It was Daniel. He wasn't even through the door before he said, "What happened? Are you all right?"

I shook my head. "Not really."

He put an arm around me and sat me down on the couch. "Tell me what happened."

I told him about my visit to see Cindy Larabee.

"That doesn't even make sense," he said. "Stan did not sell this place out from under you. He talked more than once about how he was leaving it to you." He stood. "I want to see that document."

I led him into the dining room and handed him the paper. He didn't bother reading it and flipped to the signature page like I had done.

"I knew it," he said. "That's not Stan's signature."

The relief I felt was almost overwhelming. "Are you sure?"

"As sure as I can be. I watched him sign checks numerous times over the last couple of years. He always put a little curved line underneath his name. This doesn't have it."

"Maybe he just forgot to do it."

"No way. I'll show you. Where's his will?"

I picked up the will and gave it to him.

He opened to the last page and pointed to his signature. "See here? That little line? He never forgot that. Someone copied his signature onto the sales agreement and didn't think to add the line."

"How do we prove it, though?" I asked. "This looks official."

"Believe it or not, Scott's brother is a document examiner in Hagerstown. I'll ask Scott to call and see if he can take a look at it." He called Scott and told him what was going on. Scott said he'd call his brother right away.

While we waited for Scott to call back, I showed Daniel the letter that Mr. Freeman received.

Daniel read it quickly. "Wow. MMC really wants that land."

"It doesn't make sense," I said. "If they're really considering opening the mine again, I can't imagine there's enough gold or copper to make it worth what they're willing to pay for these properties."

Daniel's phone buzzed just then and I saw Scott's name on the screen before he answered it. I couldn't hear the conversation but I knew it was good news when Daniel said, "Great." He thanked Scott, then pocketed his phone. "Looks like we're going to Hagerstown tomorrow."

* * *

Daniel picked me up at nine in the morning, and a little after ten we pulled into a public lot in downtown Hagerstown. Mark Flowers was an independent, freelance document examiner. On the ride down, Daniel told me Mark was an expert in his field who was often called on to testify in court cases. His office was in one of the historic buildings near the public library. He greeted us warmly when we entered his office.

I wasn't sure what I'd expected—maybe papers and magnifying glasses everywhere—but not this. Mark's office looked like an old library in a manor house. Wood wainscoting covered half the walls. Above it, the walls were painted a dark green. The ones not covered by bookcases, that is. His desk appeared to be mahogany, and the only things on top of it were a laptop and some kind of electronic magnifying gizmo. Mark resembled his brother but looked more like a professor. I could see why juries would immediately trust him.

"Come on in and have a seat," Mark said. "Can I get you coffee or anything?"

Daniel and I both declined.

"Scott tells me you have some questions about the authenticity of a document."

"I do," I said. "Thank you so much for taking the time to look at it. I brought all the paperwork from my uncle's estate."

"Great," Mark said. "That will give me something to compare."

I passed the folder across the desk.

Mark took a pair of reading glasses from his pocket and put them on. He smiled. "This is what happens when you hit fifty and have been staring at small print for twenty-five years." He opened the folder. "Tell me what you have here."

I explained what all the papers were—Uncle Stan's will, the deed transfer, and some miscellaneous papers. "And this is the one the attorney gave me yesterday telling me my uncle sold the orchard before he died."

Daniel had let me do the talking up till now. "I'm sure that's not Stan's signature," he said.

"Well, we'll know for sure in a bit."

Mark sounded confident, and it raised my spirits some. He wanted to know which signature we knew for certain was my uncle's. Daniel told him about the curved line Uncle Stan always put under his name.

It was hard just sitting there while he put each paper under the magnifier—some more than once. It wasn't long before he had an answer.

"You're right," Mark said. "The signature on the sales agreement doesn't match any of the other ones. Let me show you something." He put both pages with signatures side by side on the magnifier. He pointed to the sales agreement. "On this one you can see the writing is forced, like whoever wrote it didn't want to make a mistake. I see that a lot. A caregiver or family member takes checks and tries to duplicate the signature."

"That's so sad," I said.

"And unfortunately more common than you'd think," Mark said. "On the signed will, you can see the signature is natural and he put that little flourish underneath—something the forger didn't think to do."

"What about Robert Larabee's signature?" Daniel asked.

"In my opinion, it's authentic," Mark said. "It seems natural. There doesn't seem to be any hesitation or attempt to get it right."

"What do we do now?" I asked.

"I'll write up my findings and email it to you before the end of the day," Mark said.

"Be sure to include what I owe you," I said. "I can't tell you how much I appreciate this."

Mark stood and handed me back the folder. "This one's on the house. Any friend of Scott's is a friend of mine."

"Thank you so much," I said.

Daniel shook Mark's hand. "Yes, thank you."

Once outside, Daniel said, "How about some lunch?"

"I was just going to suggest that." I pointed to a restaurant across the street from the library with a nice outdoor seating area. "How about over there?"

"That'll do."

We waited for the light to change, then crossed the street. The sign on the door of the restaurant was in German. I had no idea what it said. Brian would have been able to translate it for me. His maternal grandmother had been German and had taught him the language when he was young. Daniel and I walked up a narrow hallway that opened into the main seating area. It was like stepping into a place in Bavaria. Dark woodwork contrasted with ivory-colored walls that held pictures of German scenes. Tables were covered with plaid cloths with tiny flower bouquets embroidered in the center of each plaid block. Ceramic beer steins hung from the ceiling in the bar area. A hostess seated us promptly and gave us each a menu.

"Brian would have loved this," I said after the hostess left us.

"We can go somewhere else," Daniel said. "I don't want you to be uncomfortable."

I shook my head. "On the contrary, it feels very comfortable." I smiled. "It's the first time I've been able to think how much Brian would like something and not want to burst into tears."

Our waitress came by then and we both ordered half-liters of Dunkel. We opened our menus and it didn't take long to decide to split a luncheon sausage platter. The waitress brought our beer and a bread basket, then took our order.

"What was Brian like?" Daniel asked after the waitress left.

"You don't really want to hear that, do you?"

"I wouldn't ask if I didn't want to know. You know all about me. We're friends and I'd like to get to know you a little better."

I took a sip of beer. "Brian and I met our sophomore year at Pitt. I was studying business and he was an education major."

"He was a teacher?" Daniel asked.

I shook my head. "He decided it wasn't for him as soon as he started student teaching. His dad was a teacher and he thought he should carry on the family tradition. His heart was really in construction, though. He switched to business and got his degree, then started his own remodeling company. He was so much happier remodeling houses."

"I guess that's how you learned how to wield a nail gun."

"Yep."

"So you two were together a long time," Daniel said.

"We were. A long time, but not long enough." I took another drink of beer. "Brian was very down to earth. Happy-go-lucky. Kind. He could sing. When he was working on our house, I could always tell if the project was going well or not by the songs he sang. He brought me flowers all the time for no reason. I think you would have liked him."

"I'm sure I would have."

"After I started managing the cidery in Pittsburgh, we planned on starting our own someday."

"I'll bet he'd be happy you're doing it now," Daniel said.

"He would." I cleared my throat. "But that's enough about that. What about you? I'm sure you've had someone special in your life."

"Once upon a time," he said. "Marie couldn't take living with a cop. She's now happily married to a car salesman in New Jersey."

"I'm sorry about that."

"What?" Daniel said with a smile. "That she's married to a car salesman or that she lives in New Jersey?"

I laughed. "Neither. Not exactly, anyway."

Daniel shrugged. "We just weren't right for each other. It took a while to figure it out, but we're both better off."

Our meal arrived then and conversation stopped other than discussing how great the food was. Since we had split our lunch, I had room for dessert. I chose the Kirschtorte and Daniel got some kind of chocolate peanut butter cake.

I was in a much better frame of mind on the drive back to Orchardville. It had been nice getting to know Daniel a little better. And I was more at ease about the fake sales agreement after Mark's examination. There were some big questions remaining, though. Why had Robert forged my uncle's signature, and why would that paper turn up now?

Chapter
Twenty-Two

When I opened my email the next day, the report from Mark Flowers was there. He wrote that he had sent a copy to his brother as well. I printed a copy while I made a cup of coffee, then took both out to the front porch. Blossom hopped up on my lap as soon as I sat down. I put the papers aside so I could pet her while I sipped my coffee. The forecast called for rain later in the day, but for now it was cloudy and warm with the scent of apple blossoms in the air. I felt more content than I had in a long time. I was happy. I still missed Brian, but he would have told me it was about time.

I thought about the conversation I'd had with Daniel the previous day. I was glad we'd opened up to each other. I knew Marguerite would like nothing more than for a romance to develop between me and Daniel, but for now I was happy to have him as a friend.

Blossom jumped down from my lap when Scott Flowers pulled into the driveway. I picked up the report and my empty mug and got to my feet. "Good morning," I said when he got out of the car.

He returned my greeting. "Is that the report from my brother?" He pointed to the papers in my hand.

"Yes," I said. "I haven't looked at it yet. Blossom insisted on my attention first."

"I'd like to talk to you about it," Scott said.

I invited him in and offered him some coffee. He followed me to the kitchen, where I brewed him a cup from my single-serve coffee maker, then repeated it for myself. I put cream and sugar on the table and we sat down.

"I really appreciate Mark taking the time to examine the document and write a report," I said. "It seems like he keeps pretty busy."

"He does," Scott said. "And he likes nothing more than catching these guys. He hates seeing people taken in by scammers. Why don't you read through what he sent and then we'll talk about it."

It only took minutes to read the five-page report. It was concise and matter-of-fact, spelling out his findings—that Uncle Stan's signature on the document had been written by someone else. "What do you think? What's your next step?" I asked Scott.

"After I leave here, I'm going to see Mrs. Larabee. Daniel told me the gist of the situation when he called me the other day to ask about Mark, but I want to hear it from you. I'd like you to tell me exactly what happened when you went to the law office."

"Sure." I gave him the details of my meeting with Cindy Larabee.

"So she said she found the sales agreement in a file in her husband's office."

"That's what she told me," I said.

Scott gave me a little smile. "I'm sure you have a theory about all this."

"Not much of one," I said. "I think maybe Robert kept it as a backup in case he couldn't convince me to sell."

"That's a possibility." He stood. "Thanks for the coffee."

"That's it? That's all you're going to say about my theory?"

"For now," Scott said.

"What about your theory?"

"I have several, but I'm not going to share any of them until I know more—until after I talk to Mrs. Larabee."

I sighed. I knew he didn't have to tell me anything, but it would have been nice. "Will you at least let me know how it goes?"

He said he would and I walked him to the door. I watched him drive away, then headed to the kitchen. I had a carton of eggs out of the fridge to make breakfast when I changed my mind. I'd go into town instead. Marguerite had taken her food truck to a local brewery the previous day and I hadn't told her about the latest developments. I put the eggs away and grabbed my purse.

*　*　*

Margie's Morsels was busy when I arrived. I headed for an open seat at the counter when Renee waved me over to where she and Eli were seated at a table for four.

"How about joining us?" she said.

"Thanks." I took the seat beside Renee. "Are you sure you don't mind?

"The more the merrier," Eli said.

Marguerite came out of the kitchen just then with their breakfast and set the plates down in front of them. "Hey, Kate. Coffee?"

I nodded. "Regular with cream."

"Noah will be highly disappointed, you know."

"I'll make up for it later," I said.

"You'd better," Marguerite said. "I don't want him getting bored and developing anything new again."

I laughed. "On second thought, I'll have an iced mocha."

"Good idea," Marguerite said.

When she'd left, Renee asked, "What was that all about?"

I told them about the "Kitchen Sink."

They both laughed. "Good Lord," Eli said. "He put cayenne in coffee?"

"Unfortunately," I said. "I think he's learned his lesson. At least I hope so."

Renee asked how the cidery was coming along. "I bet you're excited to open soon."

"I am."

Eli asked if they could help with anything.

"I don't think so. Not yet, anyway."

"Well, don't hesitate to ask," he said.

"I appreciate that."

Marguerite returned with my mocha and took my order for French toast. "I'll be back with this and I can take a break."

Eli stuffed the last bite of his omelet in his mouth and practically swallowed it whole. He pushed his plate aside and picked up the check. "If you ladies don't mind, I gotta run. I know at least two customers will be standing outside the shop door waiting for it to open. Not that I'm complaining."

Renee laughed. "Good thing you're not complaining. I opened every day this week. It's your turn."

He got up, leaned over, and gave Renee a kiss on the cheek. "Don't rush. Enjoy your breakfast."

After he left, Renee turned to me. "Dad said you stopped by to see him again and he showed you the letter he got."

"I did. I was surprised at how much the offer was for," I said.

"I keep telling him he should sell, but he insists on passing the farm down to me." Renee sighed. "He doesn't get that I really don't want it. I'm a craftsperson, not a farmer. I'd much rather see him live out his remaining days in comfort. He could get a nice little apartment, or move into assisted living. He won't hear of it, though."

"He has a lot of memories there," I said.

"I know he does. But it's too hard for him to keep up with everything now. We help when we can, and he has help for the farming, but . . ." She shrugged. "I try not to nag him and keep telling myself *whatever makes him happy.*"

"That's a good policy," I said. "If I can help in any way, please let me know. I really enjoy talking to your dad."

Marguerite carried my French toast out of the kitchen, placed it on the table, and took the seat across from me. "Whew. Thank goodness it slowed down. We were busy this morning."

I hadn't noticed the restaurant had mostly cleared out while Renee and I had been talking. "Where's all your help today?"

"The high school prom is tonight and apparently my usual part-timers need all day to get ready. You know—the hair salon, the nail salon, the tanning salon. I don't remember doing all that."

"I don't either," I said. "A friend and I did each other's hair and that took no time at all."

"So what's new?" Marguerite asked. "I haven't talked to you since Carl's memorial."

A lot had happened in the past two days. "Where do I start?"

"Uh-oh," Marguerite said. "That doesn't sound good."

In between bites, I filled Marguerite and Renee in about going to see Cindy Larabee, the fake sales agreement, and the appointment with Mark Flowers.

"That's crazy," Renee said. "Why would Robert forge your uncle's signature?"

"I think he had the paper in reserve to use in case he couldn't convince me to sell the orchard," I said.

The door opened just then and six people walked in. Marguerite sighed and pushed out of her chair. "I guess it's back to work. We'll have to talk more later."

Renee got up too. "I should get going. Eli will wonder what's taking me so long."

Marguerite started to walk away, then suddenly turned. "You know what we need?"

"Should I be afraid of the answer?" I asked.

"Of course." She grinned. "Tonight. It's going to be a girls' night out. Noah's playing poker with some guys and I'm not sitting home alone. What about it?"

Neither one of us hesitated. We were in. Renee said she knew just the place and she'd pick us up at seven. Considering some of the trouble Marguerite and I had gotten into as kids, part of me wondered if I should have bail money ready.

* * *

The place Renee had chosen was halfway between Orchardville and Gettysburg. It was lit up like a Broadway theater, complete with a marquee that read *Sing Sing*. "That's an unusual name for a bar," I said as we got out of the car.

Marguerite and Renee laughed.

"Not really," Marguerite said. "You'll see."

I wasn't sure I liked the sound of that. "What aren't you telling me?"

"You'll like it. I promise." Renee said.

"You'd better be right." I reluctantly followed them through the door.

There was a guy the size of a gorilla standing beside a tiny woman at a cash register. "Ten bucks cover," he said.

"I got this," Renee said, handing a credit card to the woman. "After all, this place was my idea."

After Renee got her card back and signed the screen with her finger, Mr. Gorilla held another door open for us and we went in.

"You've got to be kidding me," I said.

Marguerite nudged Renee. "I told you she'd like it."

Sing Sing was a karaoke bar. The large room was set up with round tables that sat four to six people at each. There were three areas with microphones, and screens that showed lyrics for anyone brave enough—or drunk enough—to step up to the mic. Only one of them was in use. A guy in a cowboy hat was belting out a Garth Brooks song. He didn't sound half bad.

Marguerite pointed to an empty table in that direction. "Over there."

Renee and I followed her across the room. The closer we got to the cowboy, the worse he sounded. I grabbed Marguerite's arm. "Let's sit on the other side of the room instead."

"But that's no fun," Marguerite said. "There's no one singing over there."

"Exactly," I said.

"Spoil sport."

I pointed to another table. "That one's closer to the bar."

"Besides," Renee said. "We won't have to fight the cowboy when we want to sing."

Marguerite gave in after I said I'd buy the first round. Renee only wanted a soda since she was driving.

"I don't know what I want," Marguerite said.

Just then the cowboy across the room started singing an old Alan Jackson-Jimmy Buffet song.

"Yes!" Marguerite said. "That's it! I'll have a Hurricane."

Actually that sounded pretty good. Fortunately, the bartender was up to speed on his tropical drinks and had them ready in no time. When I got back to the table, my friends were scrolling through karaoke selections. "You're not actually going to sing, are you?"

"Of course we are," Renee said. "And so are you."

I laughed. "Not a chance."

"Oh, come on," Marguerite said. "It'll be fun."

"That's not my idea of fun." I took a big swallow of my drink. "I'm perfectly content being a spectator."

Marguerite shrugged. "Suit yourself."

Five minutes later, Renee stepped up to the mic. I didn't know what to expect when she picked a famous Whitney Houston song. It didn't take long for even the cowboy to quiet down. She hit every note perfectly. She was met with thunderous applause when she finished. She bowed and sat back down.

"Your turn," Renee said to Marguerite.

"If you think I'm going to follow that, you're out of your freaking mind," she said.

"Where did you learn to sing like that?" I asked. "And why aren't you out there touring?"

Renee laughed. "I like making candles better. This is fun once in a while, but I couldn't do it all the time. It's much too stressful."

I shook my head. "But you're so good."

"Thanks," she said. "I'm serious, though. I couldn't do it all the time. I'll sing the national anthem at local ball games and things like that, but I honestly don't want to do anything other than what I'm doing."

"What else don't we know about you?" Marguerite asked.

"Plenty," Renee said. "Eli is still asking me that after all these years." She turned to me. "What's your biggest secret?"

"I'm not sure I have any," I answered. "Now, Marguerite on the other hand—"

"Oh no you don't. I'm as transparent as they come," Marguerite said.

Renee and I laughed at that, mostly because it was true.

Deadly to the Core

A little later, after a second drink, I was on my way to the restroom when I spotted a woman heading in the same direction. She was dressed in a bright red sheath dress that barely covered her backside, and her spike heels were a perfect color match. It wasn't the outfit that shocked me. I'd seen worse. What surprised me was the occupant of the dress. What was Cindy Larabee doing in a karaoke bar the day after her husband's funeral?

Chapter Twenty-Three

I was torn between rushing back to the table to tell my friends or following Cindy and seeing what she was up to. I chose the latter. She stopped in the hallway outside the men's restroom. I held back so she wouldn't notice me. Ten or fifteen seconds later, an older man came out of the restroom and she linked her arm through his. He looked surprised at first, then pleased to have a much younger woman on his arm. They headed to a table on the other side of the room. There was no way I could get closer without being spotted. Who was this man, and why was she interested in him?

I forgot about the ladies room and rushed back to our table. "You're not going to believe who I just saw," I said.

Marguerite giggled. "Someone famous? Beyoncé? Brad Pitt? If it's Brad, I want to meet him." She was a drink ahead of me and her words were slightly slurred.

"None of the above."

"Who then?" Renee asked.

"Cindy Larabee."

Marguerite craned her head. "That little bit—"

"Robert's wife?" Renee's question cut off Marguerite's words. I agreed with the sentiment, however.

"She met up with an older guy," I said. "He seemed surprised when she latched onto his arm. They went to a table on the other side of the room."

"Did she see you?" Renee asked.

I shook my head. "I made sure she didn't. I can't imagine why she'd be here the day after her husband's funeral."

Marguerite was still trying to get a look. I slapped her arm. "Stop that," I said. "She might see you."

"So?" Marguerite started to stand. "I'm going to have a chat with her. And warn the guy."

I pulled her back down. "No, you're not. If she sees either one of us, we'll never find out what she's up to. I want to know who the guy is. She might be pulling something like she did with me and the fake document."

"She doesn't know me," Renee said. "I've never met her. I could take a walk that way and see if I recognize the man she's with. What's she look like?"

"You can't miss her. Red dress, matching shoes. She's dressed like a hooker."

Marguerite snorted. "Nice side job."

I ignored her.

"Watch this," Renee said. She picked up her cell phone from the table, then strolled toward where Cindy was sitting. When she got closer, Renee put her cell phone to her ear and pretended to talk to someone. It was long enough for her to get a good look at the couple. She ended the pretend call and came back to our table.

"Well?" Marguerite asked. "Do you know the guy?"

Renee shook her head. "He looks kind of familiar—I might have seen him in town, but I don't know who he is."

I was disappointed.

"Can't you snap his picture or something?" Marguerite asked.

"Too obvious," I said. "I'll let Scott know what we saw and he can figure it out."

We watched Cindy from across the room. She didn't stay much longer, and when she got up to leave, the two exchanged a brief hug. I didn't know what to think. I was tempted to follow her but, like I'd told Marguerite, I didn't want to be too obvious. It was certainly a strange development.

* * *

First thing in the morning, I called and left a message for Scott that I had some information for him that might be important. I was just about to make breakfast when I heard knocking at the front door.

It was Daniel holding a bakery bag. "I come bearing gifts," he said.

"You have perfect timing. I was just about to scramble an egg." I took the bag from him and opened it. Bavarian cream donuts. "This is much better than eggs. I could use the sugar and some more caffeine."

He followed me down the hallway to the kitchen. "Rough night?" He sat at the table while I retrieved another cup and two coffee pods.

"Marguerite, Renee, and I went to Sing Sing."

Daniel laughed. "Really?"

"Really."

"That's something I would've liked to see. Renee has a great voice, but Marguerite can't carry a tune. How about you? What did you sing?"

"I didn't."

"Chicken?"

I opened the fridge and took out the half and half. "Absolutely."

"Did you have a good time, though?"

"I did." I handed him a cup of coffee, then made one for myself. "And wait till you hear what happened." I set some napkins on the table.

Daniel lifted a donut from the bag. "Let's see. No one called me, so you didn't get arrested. I haven't heard anything about a bar fight because Marguerite was singing off key and wouldn't give up the microphone."

"Ha, very funny." I sat down with my coffee and he slid the donut bag across the table. "You'll never guess who we saw there."

"Don't keep me in suspense."

In between bites, I told him about Cindy Larabee and the man she'd met with.

"That's really weird," Daniel said when I finished the tale.

"She's the last person I expected to see in a karaoke bar, or, frankly, any bar, especially dressed the way she was." I wiped Bavarian cream from my fingers with a napkin. "I left a message for Scott this morning. He was supposed to talk to her about the forged document, so maybe he knows what's going on."

There was a knock at the door just then, so I got up to answer it.

It was Scott. "I got your message. I hope it's not too early to stop by."

"Not at all. Come on to the kitchen and I'll make you a cup of coffee."

Scott did a double take when he saw Daniel. He glanced at me, then back at Daniel. "Am I interrupting anything?"

I felt my cheeks redden. I had a feeling Scott thought Daniel had spent the night. "Daniel just stopped by with breakfast. Help yourself." I didn't know why I thought I had to set Scott straight. Who cared whether anyone thought Daniel had slept here? I kept my back turned while Scott's coffee brewed. By then my cheek color had returned to normal.

Scott was halfway through a donut when I handed him his cup and sat down again. He swallowed and took a sip of coffee. "Tell me exactly what happened last night," he said.

I did.

"Interesting," Scott said.

"That's it? Interesting?" I asked.

"He's a man of few words," Daniel said. "The wheels are turning, though. I can tell."

"A few more words would be appreciated," I said. "What did Cindy have to say when you talked to her yesterday?"

Scott finished his donut before answering. "Nothing. I haven't been able to track her down."

"Why not?" I asked.

"She wasn't at either her townhouse or the office. Her neighbor said she left in the morning with a suitcase."

I remembered she told me she planned to go away for a few days after the funeral. I told Scott and Daniel. "If she went away, what was she doing in the bar last night?"

Scott drained his mug and stood. "When I catch up to her, that's one of the questions I mean to ask her. Enjoy your morning."

I caught the wink he gave Daniel. Scott really did think Daniel had spent the night.

Daniel got up too. "I should be going. I'll walk out with you."

"Thanks for the donuts." I followed them to the door and quickly closed it as soon as they left. My face was still warm. Did everyone think Daniel and I were a couple? I tried to push the thought of us together out of my mind, with little success. *Daniel is a friend. Nothing more*, I told myself.

I heard Brian's voice in my head telling me once again that I needed to move on and let him go. *It's way past time, babe.*

"Oh shut up," I said aloud. "What do you know anyway? You're dead."

Exactly my point.

* * *

As I walked to the cidery later that morning, I heard voices coming from the apple orchard. I left the dirt road and headed in that direction. When I got closer, I was surprised to see the Diaz brothers. I waved.

"I hope you don't mind," Gary said when I reached them.

"Not at all," I said. "I didn't think you were starting for another week or so."

Greg shrugged. "Neither one of us had anything to do today, so we thought we'd check the trees. There's only a couple that might have issues, although nothing serious."

"Can you show me which ones? Like I said before, I don't know a thing about growing fruit and I'd like to learn."

"Sure," Gary said.

I followed him and he pointed to what looked almost like a scab on a branch of one of the trees.

"This is what's called a canker," he said. "It's fairly common and we treat it by pruning."

"We haven't checked all the trees yet," Greg said, "but most are in great shape. Carl did a good job keeping them healthy."

"That's good to hear," I said. "Will you let me know what problems you find?"

"Absolutely," Greg said.

I thanked them and went on my way. While I walked, I thought about all that had happened over the last few weeks. It was hard to believe I'd only moved here a month ago. It seemed much longer than that, maybe because I still didn't have any answers to anything—Carl's murder, Robert's murder, the property sales, MMC. I also didn't understand why Carl would have taken money from Robert in the first place. Maybe he thought he'd lose his job after Uncle Stan died. I should have made it clear from the start that I'd keep him on.

I wasn't sure where else to turn to find out more about the mine and the land buyouts. First thing tomorrow I'd call Morrison Agricultural again to see if Albert Morrison was still out of town. Another person I should talk to again was Will. I wanted to find out what he really knew about the Reclamation Mine.

I still got a thrill when the red barn came into sight. I stopped for a moment to take it in. It was weird, but despite everything that had happened over the past year, I felt lucky. It was a big change since the day I moved here. Before that, I thought my life was over, but this was actually a new beginning. Not everyone got that kind of chance.

Inside the cidery, I got to work. I pulled some cider from the first batch to check it. The sample was nice and clear. I tested the specific gravity and did a quick calculation. The ABV was right where I wanted it. This batch was ready. I'd transfer it to kegs tomorrow, which meant I could move my opening up a week. I'd only have plain apple cider at the moment, but the blueberry should be ready the following week. I planned to keep adding until I had a nice variety on tap all the time.

I texted Marguerite to make sure her food truck was available this weekend, and thankfully it was. The soft opening would be on Friday evening, then the official one on Saturday. It was going to be a busy week. The next thing I needed to do was to update the website and Facebook page to let everyone know Red Barn Cider Works was the place to be this coming weekend.

I had everything updated by lunchtime and decided to take a break. I went home and ate a quick sandwich, then hopped in my Highlander and headed into town. I had a few stops to make, and first on my list was Blue and Gray Collectibles.

Will looked up when I entered the store. Instead of his usual Civil War garb, today he was wearing a Hawaiian shirt and loose khaki pants. His coloring was a cross between suntan and sunburn. "Hi,

Kate," he said. "Before you ask, I'm not ready to wear wool yet. My shoulders are the same color as a lobster."

"Ouch."

"Tell me about it. I should know better than to go without sunscreen all day at Hershey Park."

"How was it? I haven't been to an amusement park for years."

"Other than the sunburn, it was great. Did I miss anything around here?"

"Not a thing. I wanted to let you know I'm opening the cidery this weekend. The soft opening is on Friday evening, then I'm officially open for business on Saturday."

"I'll be sure to stop in," he said.

"Great. You'll get to see where I hung the map."

"I bet you found a perfect spot for it."

"It's been a hit with the few people who have seen it. I have a few questions about the map and the mine, if you don't mind" I said.

"Don't mind at all. But I don't know what I can tell you that I haven't already."

"Really? I heard you knew a lot—that you were writing a book about it." I watched his face closely. His expression didn't change, but he looked down at the counter. I should have brought Daniel with me—he'd know if Will was lying.

"I thought about it," he said. "But I never got into it that much."

"That's disappointing," I said. "I heard a rumor recently that someone was planning to reopen the mine. Have you heard anything about that?"

Will picked up a cloth and began polishing the counter. "I haven't. That's really interesting. Where'd you hear about that?"

"I don't remember, exactly."

"If it comes to you, let me know," he said. "I'd like to hear more."

"Sure thing." A customer came in then, so I said, "I've got to run. I just wanted to stop in and say hello. Don't forget to stop by this weekend."

I wasn't sure what I'd learned other than that Will definitely seemed to be hiding something. I had a feeling he knew about the possibility of reopening the mine. I decided to stop into ScentSations to see if Renee knew more about Will than she'd mentioned previously.

Renee was fixing an arrangement around a candle when I entered the shop. "I was just talking about you. Sort of," I said. I hadn't mentioned her name to Will.

"Uh-oh. That's not good."

"Nothing to worry about." I grinned. "I didn't mention anything about our girls' night out."

"Hey, I behaved myself," she said. "Have you learned any more about why Cindy Larabee was there?"

I shook my head. "I passed the information on to Scott."

"Let me know what you hear," she said. "It was kind of fun playing the spy. I want to know how it turns out."

"I will. I wanted to let you know I'm opening the cidery this weekend. The first batch of cider is ready."

"That's so exciting," Renee said. "If you need help with anything, let me know. I'll tell Eli not to make any plans for the weekend, that we're going to your cidery. I'll even mark it on the calendar so he has no excuse. He can miss whatever sports thing he was planning to watch."

I laughed. "Good."

"Oh, he'll complain about it, to be sure. But he'll survive."

"I just stopped in to see Will," I said. "I wanted to talk to him about that map I bought from him. Didn't you say he was writing a book about it?"

"Yes. About a year or so ago, that's all he talked about. He said he was going to make a ton of money."

"On the book?"

Renee nodded. "He said he found some new information and had an angle that would make it a bestseller."

"Hmm."

"What do mean by that?" Renee asked.

"It's weird. I asked him about the book and he told me he thought about writing one but he wasn't really into it."

Renee laughed and shook her head. "Sheesh. He probably decided it was too much work. My cousin is an author and she works her butt off for peanuts. Will would rather sit around and play act that he's General Grant."

"Could be," I said. "I got the feeling he wasn't telling the truth, though."

"So he'd rather lie about it than admit he changed his mind or whatever. You'd think, with his background, he'd have a ton of information to use."

"What kind of background?" I asked, thinking she'd say English or history.

"I should have mentioned it earlier," Renee said. "He has a degree in geology."

"Geology?" I said.

Renee nodded. "That's why he was so interested in the mine. He told me once that the guy who owned it shouldn't have stopped mining so soon."

"Do you think he thought there was more gold and copper down there?"

"I don't know," she said. "But between that and the fact that he's into the history of the area, he could have written something. I hate to say it, because I like Will, but he's not exactly a go-getter. He might have thought writing a book would be a piece of cake and the money would start rolling in. He once thought his Grant gig would bring in big bucks. He even tried out for a role portraying Grant in some documentary a while back. He didn't get the part. Will said he turned it down, but I suspect it was the other way around."

In other words, Will researching the mine wasn't the only thing he hadn't been truthful about.

* * *

Over the next couple of days, I forged ahead with getting everything ready for the opening of Red Barn Cider Works this coming weekend. I tried to keep focused on the task at hand, but my thoughts kept wandering. Scott had finally talked to Cindy Larabee, who of course insisted she was unaware the document had been forged. I wasn't so sure. She also denied being anywhere near the karaoke bar. She insisted on knowing who "had told such a terrible lie," but Scott refused.

It was Wednesday morning and I started a new batch of cider. I had the first batch kegged, and the second one was in a fermenter conditioning on blueberries. I hoped to have that one ready for the opening. It was a gorgeous May day. I had the sliding door open, and I could smell the blossoms on the apple trees. I'd been lucky there hadn't been a late frost so far this year and it looked like the warm weather was here to stay.

The smart speaker system I'd set up was playing one of my favorite tunes, and I was singing along while I worked. Suddenly I heard someone call out "Hello?" I just about jumped out of my skin.

A man in his late fifties or early sixties stood inside the sliding door. He had salt-and-pepper hair that was mostly salt, and a goatee. He wore khaki pants and a golf shirt that I could tell from the logo was very expensive.

I recognized him immediately. It was the man who'd met with Cindy Larabee at Sing Sing.

Chapter
Twenty-Four

"I'm sorry," he said. "I didn't mean to startle you."

I wiped my hands on a towel. "No problem. We're not open yet."

"I know," he said.

"What can I help you with?" I asked.

He smiled. "It's more like what I can do for you. I'm Al Morrison and I understand you'd like to speak with me."

Finally.

"I was out of town," he said. "In Europe, as a matter of fact."

From his tone of voice I could tell he expected me to be impressed. I wasn't. "That's nice," I said.

"What did you want to talk to me about?" he asked.

I pointed to the nearest table. "Why don't you have a seat. Can I get you something to drink? I have some pop and water in the refrigerator."

"No thank you." Morrison pulled out a chair and sat down.

I could have beat around the bush but I decided to get right to the point. "A company called MMC has been buying some of the properties around here."

"What does that have to do with me?" he asked.

"I'm wondering if one of those Ms stands for Morrison."

He looked as startled as I had been earlier when he showed up. "How did you come up with that?"

"So it's true?"

"Why would you think that?"

"Come on, now," I said. "It doesn't take a genius to figure it out. Your company and the properties bought by MMC are on land where the Reclamation Mine was located."

"Most people around here don't even remember the mine," he said. "You're new here. How did you know about it?"

I pointed to the map on the wall. I told him about buying the map and the research I'd done. "So what does the MMC stand for?"

Morrison sighed. "Morrison Mining Company."

"Why the big secret? If you're going to reopen the mine, everyone's going to know about it sooner or later."

"It's not that simple."

"Nothing ever is," I said.

He looked as if he was deciding how much to tell me. "Now that you know it's my company, I guess it doesn't matter," he said finally. "I grew up knowing the mine was there. From everything I had heard, the mine had been depleted and closed. Then about a year ago, I received a packet in the mail with some studies with ground radar images showing that there was plenty of gold and copper. The equipment is much better now than it was a hundred years ago, and this study showed how robotic equipment could retrieve the metals without disturbing much."

"Where did this study come from?" I asked.

"I don't know. Robert Larabee looked into it and assured me it was reputable."

"Why didn't you just buy the mineral rights from the property owners?"

"Robert advised me not to. It would not only cause an uproar, it would make them reluctant to sell. They'd want to cash in on the gold and copper themselves."

"Is that why you offered so much more than the land was worth?"

Morrison nodded. "It was the best way to get an offer accepted. Robert and I thought for sure everyone would be willing to sell, but that hasn't been the case. He told me when your uncle died, he never thought you'd actually move here and take over the place. And now you have this."

I didn't know what to say. For being the head of a company, Morrison didn't seem very smart. He had taken Robert's word for it that the studies were real. And he only had Robert's word for it. No second opinion. None of this set my mind at ease.

"I must have all these properties for the mining to commence," he said. "I've put just about everything I have into this endeavor. It's massively expensive. I even have new equipment in place at the factory to process the copper into a new fertilizer formula our chemists developed. I need to recoup my investment and make a profit before I lose everything."

"Maybe you should have considered that from the beginning."

"It's too late for that now."

"Why can't you just mine the properties like the Thompson's that you've already bought and leave the others alone?"

Morrison shook his head. "I need them all. What's to stop the other property owners from mining their own land? I can't make my investment back that way. What I need is for you and the others to sell to me."

"I'm not selling, Mr. Morrison."

"Give me a price. How much do you want?"

"Like I said, I have no intention of selling. My family has lived here for generations and it's been passed down to me. I can't be bought."

"Everyone has a price." He stood. "Including you." He took out his phone and typed something on the screen then passed it to me. "This is how high I'm willing to go."

The number was four times what my land was worth. I'd never have to work again. I could travel the rest of my life and still have money left over. None of which I wanted to do. "No thanks," I said.

He snatched back his phone and jammed it into his pocket. "That's my final offer. I can't go any higher. You'll be sorry if you don't accept it." He strode out the door, got into a gray Jaguar, and roared off.

What had begun as a cordial conversation had ended with a threat. At least it sounded like one to me. At first I thought he was stupid for believing in a study that was sent to him out of the blue. Now I figured his feigned stupidity was part of his plan. He and Robert had concocted this whole scheme. Had Robert had a change of heart and wanted out? And then there was Cindy. I hadn't had a chance to ask Morrison about their meeting. Despite her denial, it was obvious to me she was continuing her husband's scheme. And if Robert had really wanted out, she might have arranged for his accident along with Morrison.

Daniel drove up just then. "Who was that in the Jag? I saw him pull out in a cloud of dust."

"That was none other than Albert Morrison."

"Morrison? What was he doing here?"

I gave Daniel the details.

"That sounds like a threat," he said when I'd finished. "I'm going to have a talk with him."

I should have left that part out. I didn't need Daniel or anyone else coming to my rescue. "That's not necessary. Besides, we need to figure out the rest and Cindy Larabee's involvement. Despite what she told Scott, she had to know that document was fake. And she denied being at Sing Sing, which is also a lie."

"They both had motives to kill Robert if Robert wanted to back out. Morrison's entire livelihood is on the line. Cindy's as well."

"Exactly. But I can't help wondering what was in it for Robert. Would he get a cut? A large fee for coordinating the sales? It seems to me he took all the risks and Morrison would get all the benefits."

"What about Carl? Could he have been in on the scheme?" Daniel asked.

"I think not, but I don't know. You knew him better than I did."

"I think it was more likely he found out about it and they paid him to keep quiet. All those deposits were in cash, so we'll never know for sure. He never would have sold out Stan—or you for that matter."

I nodded. "I have a terrible feeling he was building a little nest egg in case I didn't want him to continue as manager." I sighed. "I should have told him before I even moved here that he'd always have a job."

"Don't start blaming yourself," Daniel said. "It's not your fault. Carl was an adult. All he had to do was ask you."

"I know." After Daniel left, the wheels were turning in my head. Renee had told me that Will had a degree in geology and he'd done research on the Reclamation Mine. He'd been writing, or at least getting ready to write a book until a year ago. Morrison said he had received a packet in the mail showing there was plenty more gold and copper in the ground around the same time Will had been doing his book research. Robert had supposedly verified the study. That was all too much of a coincidence. I believed the so-called study was a fake. No reputable company or even an individual would have sent real information like that anonymously through the mail. They would want a cut or perhaps a finder's fee. With what Will knew about the mine and his geology background, it wouldn't have been hard for him to write a false study. In order for Robert to verify it, he had to have been in on it from the start. He and Will concocted it and Morrison went along with it.

Until I'd been presented with the forged sales agreement, I hadn't been quite convinced Robert had been the kind of person to go to such lengths. He must have had the paper tucked away as an insurance policy in case I still wouldn't sell. And Cindy conveniently "found" the document.

I understood Morrison's motive—his company—but what were Will and Robert's? I imagined it was money. I had no way of knowing more. Scott would be able to follow the money trail, but he wouldn't do it on my say-so. He would need evidence, which I didn't have.

There was still a piece missing. I couldn't quite put my finger on it yet.

By the time I got home late that afternoon, I didn't feel like making dinner. I took a quick shower, fed Blossom, and went back into town to The Tavern. The hostess sat me at a booth and handed me a menu. I'd hardly started looking at it when my phone buzzed. I had two text messages.

The first was from Marguerite asking if I wanted to grab a bite to eat. I told her I was at The Tavern. She replied immediately saying she'd be there in a bit. The second text was from Renee saying her father told her I might be interested in something he'd found and wanted to know if I could stop by soon. I texted her back and said I could stop tomorrow.

While I waited for Marguerite, I ordered a porter from a local brewery. I'd only taken a sip of it when she arrived. I waved so she could see where I was seated.

She plopped into the bench across from me. "What a day." She pointed to my glass. "I need something stronger than that."

"Busy?"

"How'd you guess?" She flagged down a server and asked for the biggest margarita they made. "The café wasn't so bad, but my phone was ringing all day. It seems everyone wants the food truck. I'm booked for almost the entire summer."

"That's good news, isn't it?"

"Yeah, in the long run," she said. "I just didn't expect it this quickly. And don't worry—I have the cidery penciled in for one weekend a month like you wanted."

"I appreciate it. I'm hoping I'll have enough business to support it."

"Are you kidding? Red Barn Cider Works is going to be *the* place to go. I mention it to everyone."

Marguerite's drink arrived and she took a big gulp before we placed our orders. When the server left us, I told her about the visit from Albert Morrison.

"Wow," she said. "You were right all along about what that M was. Maybe you should have been a detective."

"No thanks. I'll be perfectly happy when this is all settled. *If* it's settled." I told her the rest of what I'd figured out earlier.

"Have you talked to Daniel about all this?" she asked.

"Most of it. I have to fill him in on my theory that Will is involved somehow as well."

"What about Scott? You should let him know."

"I will. Scott finally tracked down Cindy Larabee. She claims she had no knowledge the document was forged and she denied being at the bar the other night."

"That's no surprise," Marguerite said. "I'm putting my money on her. She's up to her neck in all of this."

"But how to prove it? Carl's case is at a dead end if Robert killed him, and the state police are handling Robert's accident. They may never find the vehicle that forced him off the road."

"Don't give up yet," Marguerite said. "Daniel might have some ideas." She paused with the tiniest of smiles on her face. "By the way, how are you and Daniel getting along?"

I rolled my eyes. "Stop fishing. There's nothing going on between us. He's become a good friend. That's it."

Marguerite sighed. "You disappoint me, Katie."

"Why? Brian's only been gone a year. I was recuperating for half of that. I'm still getting my bearings and trying to figure out how to be myself. Brian and I were together since college. I can't be with anyone else yet."

She nodded. "I'm sorry. I keep forgetting how long you two were together and how badly you were injured. I'll keep my mouth shut from now on."

I reached across the table and squeezed her hand. "You don't have to do that. I know you're only looking out for me. If something eventually develops, you'll be the first to know."

"I'd better be." She drained her glass and grinned. "And please let it be Daniel. I'd hate to have attempted all this matchmaking for no reason."

I laughed. "You're terrible."

"I know."

We laughed and talked all through dinner. I drove home happy and content.

* * *

On Thursday morning, I drove to the Freeman farm to see Renee's dad. I couldn't imagine what he had found that I'd be interested in. I hoped it was something for the cidery—maybe an old cider press or something to hang on the wall. Mr. Freeman was rocking on his porch just like the last time I visited. He pushed to his feet as I got out of my Highlander. He looked more frail than he had a few weeks ago.

"Come on inside," he said. "The coffee just finished brewing."

I followed him to the kitchen. There was a box on the table that looked like it was full of papers and photographs.

Mr. Freeman poured coffee from an old-fashioned percolator into two mugs. "There's milk in the fridge if you don't mind getting it."

"I don't mind at all." I retrieved the milk, then helped him with the mugs.

He eased himself into a chair. "This getting old stuff isn't for sissies. That's for darn sure."

I didn't know what to say to that. "Thanks for the coffee."

He smiled. "It keeps me kicking."

"Me too."

Mr. Freeman pulled the box closer to him. "I've been cleaning out some things. I don't want to leave too much for Renee to do when I'm gone. He pulled out a stack of black-and-white photos and slid them across the table to me. "Your grandparents used to have sort of a neighborhood picnic every year. They invited all the locals before the harvest began. My late wife must have taken these."

Most of the pictures were candid shots of everyone having a good time. The only people I recognized were my grandmother and Uncle Stan. I didn't remember my grandfather—he died when I was a toddler. I'd seen pictures, of course, but that's it. In one picture a little girl who looked to be about three years old sat on Grandma's lap. "Is that my mother?" I asked.

"I think it is," Mr. Freeman said.

"Who are all these other people?"

Mr. Freeman named them one by one. Some of the names like Thompson were familiar. "And this here was me." He pointed to a man holding a baseball glove in one hand and a bottle of beer in the other.

"You were a handsome devil," I said with a smile.

He grinned like a boy. "Still am. Or so I'm told."

We both laughed.

I took out my phone. "Do you mind if I take pictures of these?"

"How do you do that?"

"I'll show you." I lined up each photo on the table and showed him how it was done.

"Well, I'll be darned," he said. "I never knew you could do such a thing. Why don't you take the ones of your folks anyway?"

I shook my head. "No need." I tapped my phone. "I have them right here. I can always have prints made if I want to."

"Why don't you go through this box and see if there are any others you'd like."

I spent the next hour looking at pictures of the Freemans and various places in the area. I sorted them into piles according to content for Mr. Freeman. He retrieved some rubber bands from his kitchen junk drawer to bundle them up when I finished. I saved a few shots of the town in my phone. They might be nice to enlarge and hang in the cidery.

There were a dozen or so photos left in the bottom of the box, and I dumped them out on the table. Mr. Freeman picked one up.

"Lookee here," he said. "This is one from the Reclamation. Outside of it, that is."

I took the photo from him. There was a group of eight men standing in front of one of the mine entrances. I checked the back for a date; *1918—Gardner* was written in faded pencil. "Do you know who any of these guys are?"

Mr. Freeman took a close look and pointed to one of the men. "That's my grandfather. I'm not sure about the others."

"The writing on the back says *1918—Gardner*. Could one of them be Silas Gardner?"

"Maybe. I remember my grandfather saying he did go into the mine with them."

The remaining photos were also taken in front of the mine entrance. I picked up one that was an image of one man. The back of the photo read *S. Gardner—1918*. I now knew what the owner of the Reclamation Mine had looked like.

Chapter
Twenty-Five

"This is Silas Gardner." I handed the photo to Mr. Freeman. "It's nice to put a face with a name."

"It is." He slid the photo back in front of me. "You should save that one."

"Definitely." I took a picture with my phone and did the same with the other mine photos. "I can enlarge these and hang them by the map on the wall of the cidery."

"When's that place going to open anyway?" he asked. "I'm mighty thirsty."

I laughed. "You're in luck, then. Have Renee and Eli bring you tomorrow night or on Saturday. Your first drink's on me."

He grinned. "What about the second?"

"Okay, that one too. But keep it between us."

He made a locking motion on his lips. "Sealed and locked."

* * *

When I reached the cidery, Mike Thompson and one of his employees were delivering the picnic tables I'd ordered a week ago. "Sorry," he said. "I should have called to see if you were here yet."

"No problem. I'm usually here earlier but I had an errand to run." I showed them where I wanted the six tables placed inside the area where Daniel and the Diaz brothers had installed ten-foot-tall four-by-four posts. All I needed to do was hang the strings of lights from post to post.

Before he went on his way, Mike told me he and his family planned to stop by on Saturday sometime and he'd pass the word on to everyone he knew.

As soon as he left, I brought the ladder and strings of lights outside. I'd already screwed in hooks to hold the lights in place, so hanging them would be easy. I was almost done when the Diaz brothers drove up in their old Honda Accord. With the shape it was in, I couldn't believe it still ran. I suddenly had a great idea.

"Hey, you should let one of us do that," Gary said.

"You guys did the hard part," I said. "This is easy." I finished the last string and ran it over to the side of the building, then sent Greg inside to fetch the heavy-duty extension cord. When he returned, he plugged the lights into the exterior outlet. It was hard to tell in the daylight, but I thought it looked great.

Greg said they'd walked through the orchard and everything looked good, so they stopped to see if I needed help getting ready for the opening. "I don't know about Gary, but I could use another quick lesson for when we're behind the bar."

"Sure." We went back inside and I reminded them where everything was and how to run a tab for customers who wanted to. "That's all there is to it. And I'll be here all the time if you run into a problem."

"What do you need help with now?" Gary asked.

"Only one more thing," I said. "Come with me." We walked down the road to where the cabins were located. We stopped in front of

Carl's cabin. "I know you guys said you're keeping your apartment, but if you need a break during the day, or any time really, you can use this cabin. My former manager lived here. It's way too small for both of you to live here, but it would still be a nice spot to take a break." I smiled. "Or if you get sick of each other."

"That would be every day," Gary said.

Greg punched his twin in the arm. "More like every hour."

I was excited about my next idea. "That's not why I brought you here, though. I noticed your car has seen better days."

Greg snorted. "That's an understatement if I ever heard one."

I pointed to Carl's truck. It wasn't new but it was definitely an improvement over their car. "Would that help?"

They looked surprised. "Are you serious?" Gary said. "How much do you want for it?"

"Nothing. It's all yours if you want it."

Their reaction was priceless. They whooped and hollered like little kids. When they came back to earth, I told them I had to figure out how to get the title transferred since the truck had been Carl's and not mine. In the meantime, I'd give them the keys and they could use it until then.

While they settled which one of them would drive the truck and which one their car by using rock, paper, scissors, I retrieved the keys from my house. Greg won, so he drove the truck while Gary was stuck with the Honda. But they drove off as happy as can be. I was thrilled, especially for the fact that the truck started right away after sitting there for all those weeks. I believed Carl would have been just fine with my decision.

I went back to the barn after that. I checked the gauges on the tanks, then did another inventory for the weekend. I had no idea how many people would show up, but I wanted to be sure I didn't run out of anything. The only thing I might not have enough of was napkins. I decided to do a Walmart run and pick some up, along with another case or two of bottled water and some pop.

When I picked up my phone to add them to my list, I thought about the pictures I'd taken at Mr. Freeman's. Walmart had photo kiosks. I'd get prints and enlargements while I was there. And even some frames. I could have all the pictures hanging on the wall for the opening. I pocketed my phone, locked the door, and headed out.

*　*　*

Two hours later I was back at the cidery with my purchases and a drive-thru lunch. I'd bought the biggest package of napkins they had, along with some small paper plates. I already had small bags of chips and pretzels for customers to buy, which was the extent of the food I was permitted to sell with my license.

I also bought a half dozen eleven-by-fourteen frames with mats for the eight-by-ten photos I had printed. The self-serve kiosks were all either occupied or out of service, so I used the one that was employee operated. She had the photos printed and in an envelope in the time it would have taken me to print one. I was anxious to look at them but I pushed them aside to eat lunch. It was already late afternoon and I was starving.

Daniel arrived just as I finished eating. "The picnic tables look great," he said. "And you put up the lights without me."

"I did." I told him about the Diaz brothers stopping and what I'd done with Carl's truck.

"That was a great idea," Daniel said. "I wish I would have thought of it. I don't remember the rules for title transfers but I'll check for you."

I told him about my visit with Mr. Freeman and what I planned to do with the photos. I picked up the envelope and opened it. "I haven't had a chance to look at them yet." I pulled out the eight-by-tens. Daniel picked out my grandmother in one of them right away.

"You really look like her," he said.

I showed him Mr. Freeman's grandfather in the photos and then the one of Silas Gardner. "This was in 1918, two years before the mine closed," I said. "I wonder if he knew."

"Knew what?"

"Knew that he'd have to close the mine and lose everything. It's so sad."

Daniel reached over, squeezed my hand, then quickly let go of it. "He looks content in the picture. At that point, he probably thought everything would be all right."

While he spoke I studied the face in the photo. "Something about him looks really familiar, like I'd seen him before."

Daniel smiled. "You're not going to get all spooky on me and say you saw his ghost or something, are you?"

"Nothing like that. There's just something about his face. It's weird." I reached for the frames I'd bought. "I guess I've been thinking about the mine so much it's making me feel like I know him. "Well, Mr. Gardner," I said to the photo, "I hope you'll like your prominent spot on my wall, next to your map."

"How could he not?" Daniel said. "It's the best spot in Orchardville."

It didn't take long to hang the pictures with Daniel's help. They looked great. It was the perfect touch to complete that wall. After that I gave him a lesson on kegging cider. The hard apple cider I'd had conditioning on blueberries was ready a little early. Frankly, I thought it was perfect timing. I'd have two ciders ready for this weekend. If I kept up the same rate, I'd be able to add a new one each weekend just like I'd planned.

I didn't think I'd sleep at all that night because I was excited and nervous about the opening, but I slept better than I had for a long time. If Blossom hadn't jumped on me to wake me up, I probably would have slept another hour. She meowed and carried on to let me know she didn't appreciate a late breakfast. I scooped some kibble into her bowl and gave her some clean water, then made a cup of coffee.

It looked like it was going to be another gorgeous day, so I decided to sit on the porch and enjoy what was left of the morning. When I opened the front door, there was a folded sheet of paper taped to the outside. I set my mug down on the porch table. Thinking the note was from Daniel, maybe letting me know he'd stopped, I pulled it off without thinking and opened it.

The note wasn't from Daniel.

Chapter
Twenty-Six

*T*his is your one and only warning. My heart pounded and my hands shook. *Sell this place or suffer the consequences.* That was all it said, but it was enough. I went back inside and called Daniel.

He arrived minutes later and I handed him the note. "Morrison. Did you call Scott?"

I shook my head. "Not yet."

Daniel pulled out his phone and called him. "He'll be here in a few minutes. Where did you find this?"

"It was taped to the door. If I'd known what it was I wouldn't have touched it. I thought it was from you."

Daniel put an arm around me. "It's all right. We know where it came from. Morrison's not too smart to do something like this."

"He's desperate."

Scott pulled up a few minutes later. He examined the note and asked me what I had touched.

"I pulled the note off the door like this." I showed him how. "Then I opened and read it."

"What about the tape?" Scott asked. "Did you touch the tape?"

I shook my head. "I didn't."

"Good," he said. "I might be able to get a print."

"Forget the print," Daniel said. "We know it was Albert Morrison. He already threatened Kate once."

Scott looked from Daniel to me and back again. "What do you mean he threatened Kate? When did this happen?"

"Two days ago," I said. "He told me I'd be sorry if I didn't sell my property to him."

"And neither of you thought to tell me about it?" Scott said. "You should know better, Daniel."

"It's my fault," I said before Daniel could answer. "I didn't think it was a big deal."

Scott pressed his fingers to the bridge of his nose. "Start at the beginning. I want to hear everything."

We went inside and over coffee, Daniel and I took turns explaining what we had discovered about Morrison and the mine.

"This is all a convoluted mess," he said when we finished.

"I know," I said.

Scott finished his coffee and got up. "First, I'll check on Mr. Freeman since he's the other holdout. I'll have the note processed, and I'm going to have a talk with Morrison and bring him in for an interview."

"I'll go with you," Daniel said.

Scott shook his head. "Stay here with Kate." He turned to me. "You might want to think about canceling your opening until we get this settled."

"Absolutely not. Everyone is counting on me and I'm not going to cancel because of a note. If Morrison wanted to kill me, he'd have done it already." My words sounded braver than I felt, but I was not going to let fear dictate to me or ruin everything I'd worked so hard for. "Besides, he wouldn't try anything with all those people around."

Daniel walked Scott to the door, then came back to the kitchen. "No one will think less of you if you postpone the opening a week."

"I'm not canceling."

"I didn't say cancel. I said postpone. There's a difference."

"No there's not," I snapped. "I'm going through with it and everyone is going to have a great time. That's all there is to it. I don't want to hear another word about it."

"Suit yourself. But I'm not leaving your side."

"That's going to make an awfully boring day for you," I said. "I'll be fine. I don't need a babysitter. Scott will pick up Morrison and it will all be over."

Daniel didn't seem convinced. I told him again I didn't need a babysitter. "I'll tell you what. I'll text you every half hour to let you know I'm okay."

"That's not good enough."

"It's going to have to be. I'm going to get ready to go to the cidery. You"—I tapped him on the chest with my finger—"are going to pick up breakfast and meet me there. I'm starving."

I heard him mumbling under his breath as I went up the stairs. When I reached the top I heard the front door shut. I set out my clothes on the bed and headed for the shower, amazed that he'd actually listened to me.

* * *

I arrived at the cidery an hour later. I'd texted Daniel that I was on my way so he wouldn't send out a search party. I planned to spend the day making sure everything was good to go for this evening and tomorrow. I'd probably overprepared, but I was fine with that. Better than the other way around. Both the Diaz brothers were coming in this afternoon and I had asked them to bring extra ice in case I ran out.

Daniel came outside and met me as soon as I arrived. I felt like I was being protected by the Secret Service. This was ridiculous. When we got inside, he locked the door.

"You can't be serious," I said. "I am not keeping the door locked. It's my soft opening, for heaven's sake. I don't want customers thinking I'm closed."

"Until I hear from Scott that Morrison is in custody, the doors stay locked." He hadn't forgotten how to use his state police voice.

"Greg and Gary will be here in an hour."

"I'll let them in."

It was going to be a very long day if he kept this up. "Look. Morrison is just trying to scare me. If he really wanted to kill me he would have done it the day he stopped in when I was the only one here."

"You don't know that."

I couldn't put up with this any longer. "I know you mean well, but this is my business and I will do what I see fit. I'm unlocking the doors and opening the slider. It's actually easier to see anyone coming or going that way."

"I don't like it, but I see your point."

"Good. Now where's my breakfast?"

* * *

That afternoon I hung out the OPEN sign, much to Daniel's irritation. There was a steady stream of customers, many who learned through the Adams County Pour Tour site that we were now open. Friends and neighbors began to arrive later. Mr. Freeman came with Renee and Eli. He was excited to finally get his free pint of cider.

"I heard you got a threat to sell this place," he said when I finally got a chance to talk to him. "No one better leave a note on my door or they'll get a belly full of bird shot."

I believed him. I was glad Morrison hadn't visited him.

Marguerite and Noah came around five. "This is fabulous!" she said. "Didn't I tell you it would be a success?"

"It's only the first day," I said.

Noah said, "Which means it will be busier tomorrow. And when word gets out how great it is, look out."

It was so busy I hardly had a chance to talk to anyone for long. Marguerite went around telling everyone to come back tomorrow when she'd be here with her food truck.

Daniel had been on high alert all evening. I was behind the bar pouring a cider when I saw him on his phone. He came over to me when the call was finished. "That was Scott. He picked up Morrison an hour ago at his golf club. He claims he doesn't know anything about the note. Scott can't get anything out of him. I'm going to see if I can talk to him."

"Will Scott let you do that?"

"I'll give it a try, anyway. Are you okay with me leaving?"

I said I was. "I'll text you if I need anything."

It wasn't long before the crowd thinned. I received a lot of compliments on the cider and more than a few promises to return soon. The Diaz brothers left and would be back in the morning to help clean up. Noah left soon after as he had to open the café at six AM. By ten it was just Marguerite and me and three other customers.

I was wiping off the bar when I heard a vehicle pull into the parking lot. There was always a latecomer who thought they'd get a discount if they showed up near closing time. When the couple got out of the car, I was shocked to see it was Cindy Larabee and Ian Bradford. Ian headed straight for the restroom and Cindy came over to the bar.

"I'm so sorry we're here so late," Cindy said.

"What are you doing here?" I asked. "You have a lot of nerve to show up after what you did."

"I had nothing to do with that," she said.

"I don't believe you."

"Honestly, I found that paper in the files on Robert's desk. I didn't know it wasn't real."

She almost sounded convincing. "And I'm just supposed to believe what you say."

"I'm telling the truth," she said. "I do owe you an apology. I had no idea when I found that sales agreement that it wasn't legitimate. I don't know what got into Robert. I guess I didn't know him as well as I'd thought."

"How do you know Albert Morrison?"

The look of surprise on her face passed quickly. "I don't," she said. "I only know he was one of Robert's clients."

"I saw you with him."

"That's impossible," Cindy said.

"At Sing Sing."

Cindy's face reddened. "I can explain that."

"You might want to explain to the police before Morrison does. He's in custody right now."

She looked confused. "Why? What has he done?"

Marguerite motioned to me from the doorway that she was leaving. I excused myself for a minute and went to say goodbye.

Marguerite nodded her head in Cindy's direction. "She has a lot of nerve showing up here."

"She still swears she didn't know . . . well . . . much of anything."

"What did she say about the bar last Friday?"

"Nothing yet," I said. "I'm going back to talk to her. I'll keep you posted."

"Good. You sure you don't need help cleaning up?" she asked.

"I'm saving it until morning," I said. "It's been a long day, and Greg and Gary are on clean-up duty."

"Give it to the youngsters, I always say. See you tomorrow afternoon then."

The three other customers were ready to cash out, so I took care of them and said goodbye. Daniel texted that he was leaving the police department shortly and would be here soon. I texted him back that the only two customers left were Cindy and Ian Bradford.

I saw Cindy head for the restroom, then Ian came over to the bar. "Is it too late for a sample?"

"It's never too late." I filled a glass for him.

He took a sip. "This is very good."

"Thanks."

"How about showing me around before Cindy gets back?"

"There's not much to tour. Follow me."

Ian walked with me over to the fermentation tanks and I briefly explained the process. Cindy joined us then and I took them to see the map and the photos hanging on the wall. If Cindy was involved with the scheme Robert and Morrison concocted, maybe some kind of recognition would show on her face when she saw the mine photos.

Except Cindy wasn't the one who recognized something in the photos. I glanced at the photo of Silas Gardner, then at Ian. I realized why I had thought the man in the photo looked familiar. And I realized I'd been wrong about everything.

Chapter
Twenty-Seven

My face must have given it away.

Ian turned to me. "You know, don't you?"

"Know what?" I asked. I couldn't let on that I knew Ian had been behind everything. Not Robert—at least not knowingly. I had no doubt that Ian had been the one who ran him off the road. I just didn't know why and how he became involved with Morrison and Will Pearson. "Do you want to tell me what's going on?" I asked.

"Don't act stupid," he said.

Cindy gasped. "Ian, that was uncalled for."

He told her to shut up. "I'm tired of your whining."

"I'm not—I haven't." Cindy started crying.

Ian pushed her toward me, then reached behind his back and pulled out a gun.

I put an arm around Cindy. "That's really not necessary, Ian," I said. "Why don't you put it away and get out of here. I won't say a word."

"Right. You'll be on the phone to your state cop boyfriend before I'm even out of the parking lot."

"I don't have a boyfriend. I don't know who you're talking about."

"Daniel Martinez. I did recognize him that day you two were in the office. He busted a friend of mine for possession once. Where is he, by the way?"

"On the way here," I said. "He should be here any minute. He was at the police station questioning Albert Morrison."

Ian laughed. "Oh good. I'm so glad his life will be ruined now."

Cindy sobbed. "Ian, I don't understand. Why are you doing this? I thought you loved me."

"Had you fooled, didn't I? Along with your late husband. I was surprised it took him so long to figure it out. And then I had to get rid of him."

Cindy fell to her knees. "Oh, God. Oh no. Why? I don't understand." I moved to comfort her and Ian stuck his gun against my ribcage.

"Leave her there," he said. "We're going to take a walk outside and wait for Martinez. Then I'll take care of all of you."

My heart sank. I had no idea when Daniel would get here. He'd said shortly, but that could be some time. Ian would get tired of waiting and shoot me and Cindy. I needed to keep him talking. "If you're going to kill me anyway, I'd like to know why. I don't understand how all this is connected—Morrison, the mine, Robert, the land sales . . . It doesn't make sense to me."

"Fair enough. If you haven't guessed it yet, Silas Gardner was my great-great-grandfather. He lost everything to the first Albert Morrison. I wanted to make Morrison suffer like his ancestor made mine suffer. Silas Gardner killed himself and Morrison got rich off of it. And now the tables have turned. Morrison will lose everything because of his greed."

"So there's no gold or copper in the mine?"

"Not enough to make it worthwhile. It was easy to convince Will Pearson that there was actually gold down there. I talked him into creating the fake study and promised him a large cut from the proceeds."

"And Robert?"

"Robert didn't know the truth until recently. He believed what Morrison did—that there was a treasure trove underneath the ground. He was greedy enough to want to cash in. When he figured out it was all scam to bankrupt Morrison, well, he had to go."

"What about Cindy?" I asked. "What's her involvement?"

"Not that it matters, but she didn't know a thing. She loves me, so she'll do anything I ask her to do—like coming on to Morrison last week. The old guy was worried, so I sent Cindy to put his mind at ease. Looks like it worked."

While we talked I watched over his shoulder as Cindy got to her feet and headed toward us. Her steps were silent on the grass. When she heard Ian's comments, she picked up a chair that someone had brought outside and smashed it on his back.

Ian lurched forward, dropping the gun. Cindy hit him again and he fell to the ground. I dropped to my knees and grabbed the gun. Cindy hit him one more time, threw down the chair, and fell to the ground sobbing. Just then I heard a siren. Ian wasn't moving but I held the gun on him anyway until the cavalry arrived.

* * *

Ian had a lot to say after he woke up in the hospital. He told Scott everything, including that he had been the one who killed Carl. He didn't know how, but Carl had suspected something odd was going on with the offers for the land. I figured it had something to do with the topographic map Daniel and I found in his freezer. Carl took the hush money for a time but told Ian he felt guilty about it. When Carl threatened to go to the police, Ian grabbed the first thing available— my cane—and murdered him. Ian was also the one who found a generic blank sales agreement that Robert had pre-signed and entered the necessary information and forged my uncle's signature. Ian left it on Robert's desk knowing that Cindy would find it. She had been telling the truth that she knew nothing about it.

Albert Morrison had truly believed there was gold and copper to be had. I didn't know what would happen to him, but he hadn't done anything criminal. He was cooperating and would testify against Ian Bradford. Will Pearson was facing fraud charges and was also cooperating in return for a reduced sentence.

The following weekend, Daniel, Marguerite, Noah, and the Diaz brothers were helping clean up after we closed for the night. Greg and Gary left after everything was spic and span, leaving the four of us. I took four glasses, filled them with blueberry cider, and took them to the table, where I passed them out.

"What's the occasion?" Marguerite asked. "You just washed these glasses."

"It's my one week anniversary," I said. "That calls for a celebration."

"Not to mention that you single-handedly solved two murders," Marguerite said. She grinned at Daniel. "You'd think she was the ex-cop and not you."

Daniel laughed. "Would you believe I taught her everything she knows?"

"Not a chance," Noah said.

"Daniel figured it out at the same time I did," I said. "He was at the police station when he realized."

"Something I'll regret for a long time," he said. "I wouldn't have been able to live with myself if anything had happened to Kate."

Daniel put his arm around me, causing Marguerite to raise an eyebrow. I ignored her. His hand felt comfortable on my shoulder. I didn't hear Brian's voice in my head, but I felt something shift. In my heart I knew it was time to focus on the future and not the past. I'd always love Brian, but he was gone, and I had a new life to live.

"I'd like to propose a toast," I said, holding up my glass. "To old friends and new friends, to those we've lost and those we've yet to meet."

We clinked our glasses together.

"To the future."

Acknowledgments

Thank you to my wonderful agent, Melissa Jeglinski, for all her support and making things happen. And to editor extraordinaire Faith Black Ross, who insisted the manuscript wasn't as bad as I thought it was when I turned it in. That was such a relief!

Thanks to everyone at Crooked Lane who puts so much together to make a gorgeous finished product. You're the best!

Special thanks to book blogger Dru Ann Love. Her Dru's Book Musings site is a must read for mystery lovers. I'd also like to thank Lori Caswell, who arranges fabulous blog tours through her Escape with Dollycas site. I really appreciate what both of you do for the mystery community.

Thanks to Curt Henry at Tattiebogle CiderWorks, who showed me the commercial cider-making process (which isn't all that different from what I do in my kitchen, just bigger), and letting us sample some delicious products.

My cats, Hops and Lager, insist on me thanking them too. For what, I'm not sure. Maybe for the chipmunk that Hops let loose in the house. Who knows?

And thanks to my family, who keep me smiling. Special thanks to my husband, who puts up with this writing gig. Heck, for putting up with me in general, lol. I love you!